Bruce

W9-CSU-944

# TOM SWIFT AND
# HIS ATOMIC EARTH BLASTER

# THE NEW TOM SWIFT JR. ADVENTURES
## BY VICTOR APPLETON II

*The tear-gas guns brought them out of the fortress*

THE NEW TOM SWIFT JR. ADVENTURES

# TOM SWIFT
## AND HIS ATOMIC
## EARTH BLASTER

BY VICTOR APPLETON II

ILLUSTRATED BY GRAHAM KAYE

GROSSET & DUNLAP

NEW YORK PUBLISHERS

COPYRIGHT, 1954, BY
GROSSET & DUNLAP, INC.
ALL RIGHTS RESERVED

PRINTED IN THE UNITED STATES OF AMERICA

# CONTENTS

# CONTENTS

# ILLUSTRATIONS

# TOM SWIFT AND
# HIS ATOMIC EARTH BLASTER

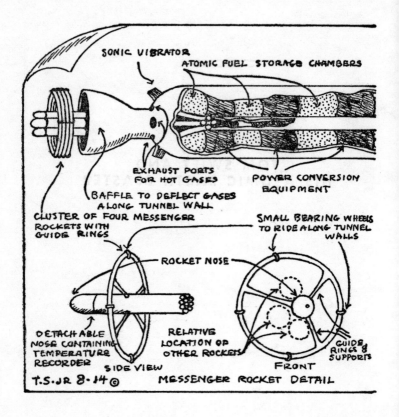

SONIC VIBRATOR

ATOMIC FUEL STORAGE CHAMBERS

EXHAUST PORTS
FOR HOT GASES

POWER CONVERSION
EQUIPMENT

BAFFLE TO DEFLECT GASES
ALONG TUNNEL WALL

CLUSTER OF FOUR MESSENGER
ROCKETS WITH GUIDE RINGS

SMALL BEARING WHEELS
TO RIDE ALONG TUNNEL
WALLS

ROCKET NOSE

DETACHABLE
NOSE CONTAINING
TEMPERATURE
RECORDER

RELATIVE
LOCATION OF
OTHER ROCKETS

GUIDE
RINGS &
SUPPORTS

SIDE VIEW

FRONT

T.S.JR 8-14 ©    MESSENGER ROCKET DETAIL

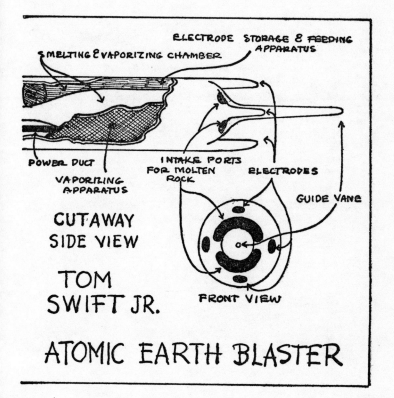

SMELTING & VAPORIZING CHAMBER

ELECTRODE STORAGE & FEEDING APPARATUS

POWER DUCT

VAPORIZING APPARATUS

INTAKE PORTS FOR MOLTEN ROCK

ELECTRODES

GUIDE VANE

CUTAWAY SIDE VIEW

FRONT VIEW

TOM SWIFT JR.

ATOMIC EARTH BLASTER

**CHAPTER 1**

# THE MYSTERIOUS STRANGERS

"MAN, look at this earth blaster go to town!" yelled Bud Barclay from the cab of a big tractor trailer.

"Speed her up a bit!" urged Tom Swift as he jogged alongside it.

The blond, rangy young scientist and his husky, dark-haired pal were testing Tom's latest invention—an atomic-powered earth-digging machine, mounted on a platform above the truck's cab. Tom hoped to use his invention for road and bridge construction work and for drilling tunnels.

As Bud gunned the engine, the grinding hum of the earth blaster rose to an ear-shattering roar.

The machine looked like a gigantic torpedo and was comprised of three main parts. Mounted to a heavy swivel base was a long, gleaming steel cylinder which could be tilted in any direction. It housed a compact atomic pile to power the implement. Ex-

1

tending from the cylinder was a narrower shaft, containing transmission gears to conduct the power to the nose end of the shaft. This end was armed with a pair of revolving steel discs which could chew into the hardest rock.

As the machine bored into the ground, Tom suddenly noticed that Bud was swerving to the right.

"Hey, watch where you're going!" he warned.

The young inventor had obtained permission from a farmer to dig on a vacant section of partially wooded land adjacent to the right of way for a water conduit. Tom had chosen this spot, a quarter of a mile off the highway near Shopton, because its rocky formation would provide a better test than the Enterprises' loamy ground.

Unknowingly, Bud was now steering toward the water company's right of way!

As the huge truck rumbled along, the machine plowed a deep trench in the ground. A steady stream of pulverized dirt and rock spewed out of the rear of the cylinder into the trailer.

Tom sprinted faster in a frantic effort to catch up with the lurching monster.

"Hold it!" he yelled. "Stop the truck! There's a water conduit over there!"

But the thundering roar of the earth blaster drowned out his voice.

The next moment, Tom heard a loud clash of

metal on metal. A split second later a geyser of water shot up one hundred feet into the air!

Hastily Bud jammed the truck into reverse and backed away from the drenching outburst. But it was too late—the damage was done!

"We've hit an aqueduct!" Tom shouted, as he drew up alongside. "Hand me the walkie-talkie!"

In stunned silence, Bud reached back, grabbed the walkie-talkie off the cab shelf behind him, and passed it out to Tom. Quickly Tom made radio contact with Swift Enterprises.

"We've had an accident," he explained. "Our digging machine broke a conduit. Phone the water company right way and get a repair crew out here pronto!"

Within five minutes, an emergency crew from the Enterprises plant arrived on the scene. It was headed by Hank Sterling, square-jawed chief engineer of the Swift patternmaking division and general trouble shooter for the outfit.

By now, however, the geyser had stopped, indicating that the water company had either shut off pressure at the pumps or closed a valve somewhere in the system.

As Tom pointed out the damage, other vehicles began to pull up at the scene—two police cars, several fire trucks, and a number of private cars containing curious townspeople.

"Won't take long to fix," observed Hank, looking down into the pit. He immediately began barking orders to his men, who had already unloaded welding equipment and a

*It was too late—the damage was done!*

section of replacement pipe from the repair truck.

Meanwhile, Tom turned his attention to the police and firemen, who were doing their best to keep the crowd in check.

"Think you can handle the situation?" asked the burly chief in charge of the fire trucks.

"I'm quite sure we can," Tom said. "Sorry you had to call out all this fire equipment."

"Don't worry about that," replied the fire chief. "We always find it's safer to get there first and ask questions later."

"Maybe you won't find it's so easy to handle Old Man Greenup," remarked a uniformed police ser-

*"We've hit an acqueduct!" Tom shouted*

geant. He jerked his thumb toward a long, black limousine which had just pulled up a moment before.

Tom saw a man with iron-gray hair climb out of the car. Frowning, he hurried toward them with decisive strides.

"Who's he?" Bud asked in a low voice.

"The president of the water company," Tom said quietly, keeping his eyes fixed on the newcomer. He knew that he was in for trouble, and hoped he could avoid involving his father and Swift Enterprises.

Greenup's face was red with anger.

"So you're the young man who's responsible for this mess!" he snapped at Tom.

"It was strictly an accident, Mr. Greenup," explained Tom respectfully. "I'm sorry if we caused any inconvenience, but it—"

"Inconvenience!" Greenup roared. "Do you realize that was the principal transmission line you burst? We had to stop the pumps and shut off water to the whole community! Suppose a bad fire broke out. What would the fire department do for water? And what about the Shopton Hospital—suppose they need water there!"

Sensing trouble, the spectators crowded closer.

"I understand all that, sir," Tom said. "I realize that an accident of this kind could lead to a mighty serious situation. But our men will soon have the main repaired, and I can promise you that Swift Enterprises will pay for any damage."

"Never mind all that!" Greenup retorted irritably. "How did it happen in the first place?"

"It was my new earth-digging machine," explained Tom. "We accidentally plowed into the water main."

"So that's it! More of your crazy contraptions!" stormed Greenup. "In my opinion, you're a public menace and your father should be haled into court for not keeping you under better control!"

Bud Barclay shouldered his way forward. Tom saw that his friend was about to blaze back angrily, and put a firm hand on Bud's muscular arm.

"Please keep my father out of this, Mr. Greenup," Tom replied evenly. "If you think my inventions haven't benefited anyone, that's your privilege."

"Well, don't think it's *your* privilege to go around smashing up public property!" snapped Greenup.

Hearing Greenup's angry voice, Hank Sterling left the repair crew and stepped over.

"We'll have your pipe fixed in half an hour," he said.

Greenup snorted. "It's bad enough even when we don't have to cope with trouble like this! The water supply was dangerously low before this happened. We need at least fifty percent more capacity, especially during these dry summer months."

Tom recalled that a town order recently had been issued banning the sprinkling of lawns during the peak hours of the day.

"That's no reason to get sore at us!" Bud declared.

But Greenup had not run out of verbal ammunition. "If it weren't for Swift Enterprises and the Swift Construction Company," he said, scowling, "there wouldn't be a water shortage!"

"How do you figure that?" Tom challenged.

"In the past few months, the construction plant has boosted water consumption between eighty and one hundred thousand gallons a day. By adding new workers to the payroll, you've drawn hundreds of new families into Shopton."

Bud grinned. "The Chamber of Commerce likes it!"

"Maybe the answer is to bring in more water," Tom suggested quietly.

"We're planning to do that," Greenup said importantly. "We intend to tunnel through Pine Hill and tap Silver Lake. But all that takes time. We can't hope to have that lake water piped in before next summer."

After a few more grumbling remarks, he wandered off to inspect the work of the repair crew. The men, stripped to the waist, were dripping with sweat as they labored under the hot August sun.

"Say, pal, I'm sorry I got you into all this," Bud apologized, an embarrassed look on his face.

"Forget it," Tom replied. "Greenup's been peeved at Swift Enterprises for quite a while. He tried to make trouble for Dad at the last meeting of the Town Council."

"My hands were so sweaty from excitement that they slipped off the steering wheel and the truck got away from me."

"By the way, where did you leave it?" Tom asked.

"Over there by that—" Bud broke off abruptly, a bewildered expression on his face. "Holy smoke, it's gone!"

"What!" Tom whirled around in the direction his friend was staring.

"I parked it over there by that tree," Bud faltered, pointing to a spot about fifty yards from the place where the main had been broken. "But it's not there now!"

"Someone must have moved it!" Tom exclaimed.

Hastily he questioned the police and firemen, then went over to speak to Hank and the repair crew. In the excitement, no one had noticed what happened to the truck with the atomic earth-digging machine.

As he rejoined Bud, Tom ran his fingers worriedly through his blond crew cut. "Come on," he told his friend. "Let's look for tread marks."

The two boys easily picked up the trail and followed it for about thirty yards toward the highway. Then it vanished on a stretch of hard, sun-baked ground.

"Maybe we can pick out the marks again on the sandy shoulder of the highway," Bud suggested. "We know the tread pattern."

"You go ahead and look," Tom ordered. "I'll try the other direction, among the trees."

As he ran toward the grove, Tom puzzled over the mysterious disappearance of the earth blaster. What was back of it?

Among clumps of coarse grass and weeds, Tom found marks of heavy tires. He followed the trail without any thought that danger might lie ahead.

A few moments later the young inventor came in sight of the truck itself. A stranger was seated in the cab with a sketch pad resting on the steering wheel. Apparently he was making notes and drawings of the earth blaster!

"Hey, you!" shouted Tom angrily. "What's the big idea, stealing our machine?"

The stranger looked up with a startled expression, then jerked open the door and jumped down on the opposite side of the truck.

He made a dash for the wooded area, but Tom quickly caught up with him and grabbed him by the coat collar.

As the tall stranger spun around, Tom saw that he was gaunt and hollow-cheeked. His green eyes glittered with hatred. One hand whipped inside his coat and came out again clutching a snub-nosed blue-steel automatic.

Tom had seen the move in time. With his left hand he grabbed the man's wrist. The stranger tried desperately to wrench his gun hand free.

For a moment the two struggled furiously. Tom,

*Tom fought desperately, but resistance was futile*

though not so tall as his opponent, had the wiry, muscular strength of a well-trained American athlete. He twisted the man's wrist farther and farther until he gasped in pain and dropped the weapon to the ground.

"Now you're going to tell me what this is all about!" Tom shouted angrily. "And then I'm—"

His words were choked off as he was grabbed from behind. Turning his head, he saw that his assailants were two rough-looking men.

Tom fought desperately, but resistance was futile. Each man held one of his arms tightly.

"What'll we do with him?" one of the captors asked, breathing hard from the effort to hold the prisoner still. The other man had clamped one hand over Tom's mouth, so that he could not call for help.

"I think I noticed some rope in the truck," replied the gunman in a deep voice that had a foreign accent. "Hold him while I get it. Then tie him to that tree."

A moment later he returned with the rope. Tom was shoved back against the tree and lashed tightly to the trunk. As one of the men knotted the rope, the other gagged the young inventor with a bandanna handkerchief.

"Good! Now let's get out of here!" said the man with the foreign accent.

With his two henchmen at his heels, he ran back to the truck.

As Tom watched in helpless fury, they climbed aboard. One of the strong-arm men took the wheel and gunned the engine into life.

Then, with a clashing of gears, they roared away from the scene, taking Tom's amazing, new atomic earth blaster with them!

**CHAPTER 2**

# ATOMIC SPY

TOM WRITHED and twisted to free himself from his bonds. But instead of loosening the ropes, his desperate efforts only made them cut more painfully into his arms.

Failing in this attempt, Tom concentrated on working the gag out of his mouth. By pushing the bandanna with his tongue, he tried to force it out from between his teeth. But again his efforts were futile.

Almost three-quarters of an hour after the young inventor had been taken prisoner, he heard voices shouting his name. Then came the sound of footsteps in the underbrush. A few moments later Tom's heart pounded with relief as Bud Barclay sprinted toward him, followed by one of the repair crew.

"For the love of Mike!" Bud exclaimed, as he ripped away the bandanna. "What happened to you?"

"Get these ropes off me first and I'll tell you later!" said Tom, who was filling his lungs with deep breaths of fresh air.

The repair crewman pulled out a jackknife and handed it to Bud. "Here, use this," he said. "I'll go tell the others we've found him."

As Bud cut the ropes, he said, "You really had us worried, genius boy! At first I figured you were just trekking all over the map, looking for the truck. But after we waited half an hour, and you still didn't show up, we decided to organize a search party."

"It's a good thing you did. I was nearly choked."

By the time Bud finished unwinding the rope from Tom's legs and arms, the other searchers came up in the jeep. Among them were Hank Sterling and Harlan Ames, chief security officer at Swift Enterprises.

Tom quickly told them everything that had happened.

"That foreigner you saw taking notes in the truck—" questioned Ames, "what did he look like?"

"He was very tall," Tom said. "Must have been over six feet. And he was gaunt and lanky. But the queerest thing about him was his eyes."

"Queer in what way?"

"They were light green and sinister-looking." Tom looked grim as he recalled the attack. "Boy, I'll never forget the look he gave me when I grabbed him by the collar!"

Tom then described the two other assailants, remembering that one man had a slight scar over his left eyebrow and that the other wore a fancy stone-studded belt buckle.

Harlan Ames reached inside his coat and pulled out a small photo. "See if you recognize this picture," he said, handing it to Tom.

"Why, that's the fellow I grabbed!" Tom exclaimed. He glanced at Ames with a puzzled expression. "Who is he? And why are you carrying his picture?"

"He's a dangerous foreign agent," said Ames. "This photograph was circulated to all law-enforcement agencies by the FBI. They suspect Bronich of stealing United States defense secrets for the Kranjovian government."

"What kind of defense secrets?" Tom asked, concerned about this new aspect of the mystery.

"Top atomic secrets," Ames replied.

Bud gave a low whistle. "Tom! No wonder Bronich was so anxious to get the low-down on your earth blaster!"

"I still don't get it," Tom admitted ruefully. "It's true that the blaster is powered by atomic energy. But there's nothing very secret about that. Every nation on earth must know how to construct an atomic pile by this time."

"Maybe so," agreed Ames, "but none of them

knows how to harness atomic energy in the form of an earth-digging machine like yours."

"But the earth blaster is for peacetime use," Tom protested. "It's not a weapon that could be used for fighting a war."

When Ames pointed out that the blaster might be adapted to military uses, Bud added:

"Besides, those rats would steal the tin cup from a blind man if they figured it might help them!"

"I guess you're right," Tom agreed in a troubled voice. "Anyhow, they must be up to no good or they wouldn't have taken it."

"The question is, what are we going to do about it?" Bud pondered.

Tom thought for a moment. "How about that break in the water main? Is it repaired yet?"

"All fixed," said Hank. "Old Greenup had nothing more to gripe about, so he went back to town."

"Thanks, Hank. You and your men return to the plant. The rest of us will try to pick up a lead on Bronich and his two henchmen."

Sterling gave a friendly salute and left, as Tom, with the help of Bud and Ames, resumed the job of following the tire marks. The prints wound through the grove of trees and emerged on the other side, where the ground sloped down to a winding dirt road.

"Not much hope of catching them now," muttered Bud. "They're probably miles away by now."

"Maybe we can still find the earth blaster," Tom said hopefully. "From what happened, I don't think they intended to steal it in the first place—they just wanted to make sketches of it while we were busy with that broken water main."

"I think you're right," Ames agreed. "They'd never stand a chance of getting away with it, once a police alarm was sent out. And they certainly won't find it easy to hide something as big as a tractor truck with that machine on it!"

With Bud at the wheel of the company jeep, the three followed the tire tracks made by the truck on the dirt road. Two miles farther, near a bend in the Indian River, Tom gave an excited cry.

"Look!" he shouted, pointing to the right. Close to the riverbank stood the truck and the atomic earth blaster!

Bud slammed on the brakes and the jeep skidded to a halt. In a mad dash Tom led his two friends to the riverbank.

"They must have had a boat cached here!" exclaimed Bud. "You can see where they shoved it into the water when they made their getaway!"

But Tom was more interested in the earth blaster. He let out an angry groan when he saw that the machine had been partly disassembled.

"Anything missing?" Ames asked nervously.

"Yes, the secret activator mechanism!" Tom cried. "The most important part of the whole design!"

Bud slammed his fist against one of the heavy truck tires. "Those dirty, sneaking thieves!" he raged. "And after all the work you've done on this blaster!"

"Don't worry," Tom said grimly. "They won't get away with this. I'll find Bronich and put him behind bars, if it's the last thing I do!"

The others knew that Tom's words were no idle threat. In the adventures, *Tom Swift and His Flying Lab* and *Tom Swift and His Rocket Ship,* the youthful inventor had turned the tables on other foreign agents seeking to harm the free world. And in *Tom Swift and His Jetmarine,* he had brought a gang of modern pirates to justice. His most recent adventure, *Tom Swift and His Giant Robot,* concerned the capture of a crazed scientist, bent on destroying Tom's robot and his father's atomic energy plant.

Tom drove the earth blaster back to the plant, with Bud and Ames as his escort.

"I'll alert the FBI and the police right away," the security chief promised as the gate shut behind them.

With the machine safely housed in Tom's experimental laboratory, the two boys drove back to a boathouse on Indian River and rented a fast powerboat. They cruised up and down the river, scanning every cove and dock for Bronich and his men, until darkness fell and they had to give up.

"They made a clean getaway," Tom said, discouraged, as he and Bud returned the boat. "I had hoped to tell Dad we caught the rascals."

At home that evening, after giving his father a quick report on the day's events, Tom ate a late meal by himself. The rest of the family had finished dinner some time earlier.

Rather than sit alone in the dining room, Tom preferred to eat in the big, cheerful kitchen of the Swift residence. As his dainty, attractive mother served the food she had been keeping warm on the gleaming white kitchen range, his seventeen-year-old sister Sandra plied him with questions about the day's events.

"Does this mean your earth blaster is ruined?" the blond, blue-eyed girl inquired anxiously.

"No, but it will hold us up a bit," said Tom. "It'll take at least a week to build a new activator and get our working model back in operation."

As he went on to explain the details, Mrs. Swift smiled at her son proudly. Even though most of the time she did not understand the technical aspects of Tom's and his father's work, she always listened attentively when they talked about it.

After supper Tom rejoined his father. Mr. Swift

was seated in his comfortable private den, a large room on the first floor of the house, which opened onto a terrace through French doors.

"Any word yet from Ames about that atomic spy?" Tom asked.

"Not yet. But the State Police and the Coast Guard have joined in the search, so it should be only a matter of time."

"I sure would like to find out why that fellow Bronich wants the earth blaster!" Tom went on.

As Mr. Swift discussed the matter with his son, his thoughts went back to some of the hair-raising adventures he had gone through in connection with his own youthful inventions.

Tom had inherited his father's scientific genius and resembled him closely. Both had the same keen, deep-set blue eyes, but Tom was the taller of the two.

"By the way," remarked the elder inventor, "Uncle Ned is coming over tonight. He wants to talk over plans for manufacturing your earth blaster. He said he had some problems to take up concerning our jet plane production, too."

A few minutes later they heard the sound of a car on the graveled side drive.

"That must be Uncle Ned now!" Tom exclaimed, jumping up from his chair. "I'll go let him in."

Ned Newton was his father's oldest and most loyal

friend. He was also the business manager of the Swift Construction Company, which had expanded to nationwide importance under his guiding hand.

Tom met him at the front door and led him back to Mr. Swift's den. The two old friends greeted each other warmly. In the old days, before Tom was born, Ned Newton had helped Tom Swift Sr. defeat many dangerous and unscrupulous enemies.

When Uncle Ned was seated in a comfortable chair, he turned to the younger Swift with a twinkle in his eye. "I hear you had a slight brush with Mr. Greenup."

Tom grimaced. "I just hope it doesn't lead to trouble with the Town Council."

"You let me worry about that," Uncle Ned replied, and added with a chuckle, "His bark is worse than his bite. I know—I've handled that old curmudgeon before."

"Just the same, this water problem is getting serious," said Mr. Swift. "If the water company doesn't find an answer pretty soon, we may have to curtail operations at the plant!"

The two older men and Tom discussed this situation and other production problems facing the Swift Construction Company.

"In my opinion," remarked Uncle Ned, "the worst problem facing us is a threatened shortage of good iron ore. Without ore, the mills can't produce steel. And that could lead to a mighty dangerous situation for the whole free world!"

"What about the Ungava range up in Labrador?" asked Tom.

"That will help," Uncle Ned admitted. "But it won't supply all the world's needs and in time it may peter out just like the Mesabi did." He puffed thoughtfully on his pipe, then said, "Tom, can't you figure out a new source of high-grade iron ore?"

The young inventor was staring intently off into space. It wasn't the first time that he had given thought to this particular problem.

"I can do better than that," he said finally. "I can name you a source of *pure iron.*"

"Where?"

"The center of the earth."

Uncle Ned's eyebrows shot up in surprise. "Impossible! No one could tap that!"

Tom disagreed. An amazing idea had just occurred to him.

"I think I could do it," he said quietly.

# CHAPTER 3

## DANGER SIGNAL

UNCLE NED and Mr. Swift stared at the young scientist in amazement.

"Are you serious?" Uncle Ned asked.

"Very much so," Tom replied.

"Serious about what?" put in a girl's lively voice.

"Oh, come on in, Sandy. You too, Mother."

Sandra and Mrs. Swift had just finished clearing away Tom's dishes in the kitchen and had come to join the others. Instantly Tom drew up a chair for his mother, while Sandy perched on the arm of Mr. Swift's chair.

"Tom was just telling us he has an idea for tapping pure iron from the center of the earth," Uncle Ned explained. "I must say it seems a little far-fetched, even from Tom."

"If my brother says it's possible, you can bet on it!" Sandra declared.

24

"Thanks, Sandy," Tom said, grinning. "I hope I can convince everyone else that easily!"

"What is it you have in mind, son?" Mr. Swift inquired.

"Well, to begin with," Tom said, "scientists are agreed that the center of the earth is molten iron."

"The entire core of the earth is molten iron, isn't it?" Uncle Ned asked.

"No one knows for sure," Tom replied. "However, my own hunch is that the inner core is solid iron, with a layer of molten liquid in between that and the earth's outer crust. I base my theory on the shape of the earth and the fact that it rotates on a fairly stable axis."

"You may be right," Mr. Swift agreed thoughtfully. "That theory agrees with most estimates of heat at the earth's core."

"Anyhow," Tom went on, "it's certain that if we burrow down below the earth's crust, we'll strike molten iron."

"Goodness, it sounds as if you'd have to go miles down!" his mother exclaimed.

Tom nodded. "That's true. But there's one place where I believe the molten iron is much closer to the surface than anywhere else on earth."

"Where's that?" Sandy asked. She was listening eagerly, her chin cupped in her hands and her eyes wide with interest.

"At the South Pole," Tom replied.

There was a stir of surprise as the young inventor went on to explain his reasons.

"For one thing, it shows up in the ground temperature. You see, up in the north polar regions, the soil is covered with a solid layer of permafrost all year round. But down south, in the Antarctic, you find spots that are warm and free from snow.

"Also, magnetic flux lines enter the earth near the South Pole."

"Those are pretty good arguments," Mr. Swift conceded. "But your mother is still right. Even at the South Pole, that molten iron must be several hundred miles down. And that would take a lot of digging, even for your atomic earth blaster."

"It would leave quite a pile of dirt, too, I should think," put in Sandra with a laugh.

Mr. Swift pulled a small slide rule out of his pocket and did some hasty figuring.

"Suppose you dug a pit three feet in diameter," he said. "For every hundred miles you went down, you'd haul up enough dirt to cover six square city blocks and piled three times as high as the Empire State Building!"

"Golly!" Sandy gasped, and for the first time expressed some doubts about her brother's plan.

But Tom had a solution. "We could get around that by changing the design of the earth blaster."

"How?" his father asked.

"Instead of using the atomic energy to grind up the dirt and rocks, we could use it to power an electric smelter. This would release gaseous oxygen from the melted rock. And the gas in turn would billow up the shaft, carrying the particles of ore dust with it, so we wouldn't need a conveyor."

Mr. Swift tugged at his lower lip and nodded thoughtfully. But Uncle Ned shook his head.

"Even if your idea is sound, think of the tremendous expense involved. I'm afraid we could never finance such a venture."

"I'm sure that the government would help out on the cost," said Tom. "Especially if we invite their scientists to go along on the expedition."

"There's one other objection, Tom," his father put in. "Suppose you did strike that molten iron. You'd have every government that ever staked a claim at the South Pole insisting the ore belonged to them too."

Frowning, Tom got up and paced around the room.

"Well, Dad, that's a question the United States government would have to settle. But one thing I'm sure of. No government that *hasn't* staked a claim at the South Pole should be allowed to drill there!"

"You mean like Kranjov, for instance?" asked Sandy.

"Right!"

At that moment there was a loud buzz, accompanied by a whining, growling sound, as though a pack of watchdogs had suddenly caught a scent of danger.

"The alarm system!" cried Sandy, jumping up from her chair. "Someone must be trying to break into the house!"

"You and Mother stay here!" Tom declared.

With the two older men, he made a dash to check on all doors and windows.

The entire house and grounds were surrounded by a magnetic field. Any person entering this field automatically set off the alarm system, unless provided with some kind of deactivator mechanism.

The Swift family and their friends all wore little neutralizer coils in their wrist watches for this purpose. But prowlers or unexpected visitors unknowingly always signaled their presence by touching off the alarm.

Next, Tom flicked a switch near the front door and immediately the grounds were flooded by the glare of powerful spotlights, arranged to cover every bit of the property. Tom had installed them after a previous burglary attempt.

"This should flush anybody hiding in the shrubbery," Tom said, poking around the bushes with his father and Uncle Ned. The young inventor found several sets of footprints on the grass, but they faded out and led nowhere.

"Let's use the bloodhounds," Mr. Swift said.

The two dogs, Caesar and Brutus, were kept in kennels behind the garden. Straining at the leash, under Tom's and his father's control, they made a complete circuit of the house and grounds.

But even the bloodhounds failed to locate the intruder. Puzzled and uneasy, Tom and the two older men returned to the house. Mrs. Swift and Sandra were waiting for them in the den.

"Who was it?" asked Sandra.

"I don't know. He got away," Tom replied in a worried tone of voice.

When they resumed their interrupted conversa-

*They made a complete circuit of the grounds*

tion, Uncle Ned asked for more details about Tom's plan.

A few minutes later they heard someone tapping on the study window! Mrs. Swift gave a startled gasp.

"Take it easy, Mumsy." Tom laughed, hoping to reassure her. But he himself felt uneasy as he got up to open the Venetian blind and look out.

The window tapper was Bud Barclay!

Tom gave an inward sigh of relief. "Come around back to the terrace!" he shouted. "I'll let you in through the French doors."

"Hope I didn't startle you folks," said Bud, as he entered the room. "It was awfully stupid of me, but I forgot to wear my neutralizer wrist watch."

"What!" Tom cried.

Bud looked at his friend in surprise. "Well, for Pete's sake, don't get so worked up about it. Anyone can make a mistake!"

"You don't understand," Tom said. *"The alarm system didn't go off this time!"*

"Huh?" Bud stared. "You mean I didn't set off the alarm, even though I wasn't wearing the coil?"

"That's right," said Tom. "And the funny thing is, the alarm *did* go off about twenty minutes ago, but we couldn't find anyone."

"I think perhaps we'd better investigate further," Mr. Swift said, rising.

This time, Tom took a small wrench from his pocket and held it up close to the dial over the front door. The dial was supposed to react to the presence of metal and thus reveal any concealed weapons carried by visitors. But the fluctuating needle remained perfectly still.

"There's your answer," Tom announced grimly. "The whole alarm system is dead!"

# CHAPTER 4

# A PERILOUS EXPERIMENT

WHAT HAD WRECKED the alarm system? Tom wondered. Was it accidental, or a case of deliberate sabotage?

The young inventor ran downstairs to his laboratory workshop in the basement and came back a moment later with a kit of electrical tools. Then he began to make a complete inspection of the electromagnetic alarm circuits. In a few minutes he had the answer.

"It was sabotage, all right! Someone shorted the winding on this solenoid. And in my opinion, it was done by a clever technician—someone who knew exactly what he was doing!"

"Bronich!" exclaimed Bud.

"Could be." Tom put his tools back in the kit.

"Judging by the job he did on the earth blaster, he must be a trained engineer. All we have to do now is find him!"

"Which may not be so easy," Uncle Ned observed in a worried voice. "At least not tonight. We've already been over the house and grounds."

"We'd better make the rounds again—just to play safe," Mr. Swift said. "And we'll use the bloodhounds."

This time, they split up into two teams. Tom and Bud covered half the grounds with Caesar, while Mr. Swift and Uncle Ned searched the other half with Brutus.

But again they found no intruder. A short time later Uncle Ned and Bud said good-night and left. After they had gone, Mr. Swift turned to his son.

"Perhaps it might be wise to repair the alarm system before we turn in. We could have a guard sent over from the plant, but I'd feel safer with our own system in operation."

"Good idea," Tom agreed. "It's going to take some time, though. When that solenoid was shorted, it blew the whole main circuit."

"This time we'll put in a stand-by circuit to take over in case the main system fails."

It took Tom and his father most of the night to design and install the new system. But finally they were able to snatch a few hours' sleep.

Over a late breakfast the next morning, they talked again about the possibility of a South Pole expedition in search of iron.

"I have to fly to Washington today, anyhow," Mr. Swift announced. "While I'm there, I'll sound out the authorities about government backing."

"I sure hope that you can sell them on the idea!" Tom said. "In the meantime, I'll get back to work on the atomic blaster. I believe I can use my present design as the basis for a much more powerful machine to penetrate the earth's crust."

After breakfast father and son drove to Swift Enterprises. Here, in a cluster of buildings and airstrips sprawled over a four-mile-square enclosure, their scientific ideas were developed.

Tom said good-by to his father at the main gate and hurried to his own private laboratory. To get in, he took an electronic key from his pocket, dialed the proper wave length, and beamed it at the lock. The door flew open.

The laboratory was equipped for all kinds of experiments. It contained an electron microscope, chemical supplies and glassware, a small electric smelter for metallurgical work, and a variety of other apparatus.

Seated on a stool in front of his workbench, Tom quickly applied his thoughts to the job of altering and improving his original blaster design.

Where to begin?

For one thing, he must adapt the cooling system, invented for his giant robot, for use in the earth blaster. This system used a highly paramagnetic fluid which was alternately magnetized and demagnetized. The fluid was circulated through the vacuum tubes inside the robot and controlled by a thermostat to maintain an ideal working temperature of 96.4° Fahrenheit.

A similar system would be needed to protect the instruments in the earth blaster from overheating. A hundred miles down, the blaster would have to operate at temperatures of several thousand degrees —hot enough to shrivel a human being to ashes!

"And speaking of instruments," mused Tom, "she'll need a gyroscope, too." He smiled at the thought of what might happen if the machine ever veered off course. "It might burrow into some other country's territory and swipe their ore!"

Two hours later, while Tom was busy with his slide rule working out structural details of the new blaster, he became aware of voices outside the laboratory window.

One voice was that of Bud Barclay, the other Tom recognized as Chow Winkler's. Chow was a former chuck-wagon cook from the Texas Panhandle, whom Tom and his father had first met while they were engaged in atomic research in the Southwest.

Chow had become so attached to the Swifts that he had accompanied them back to Shopton and taken over the job of chef on expeditions.

"What's young Tom up to now in that lab o' his?" Chow was asking.

"Why, haven't you heard?" Bud replied. "He's inventing a pair of shoes that leave no footprints!"

A moment later Bud and Chow entered the laboratory. The cook was a short, bronzed, roly-poly man, with bowlegs and a round head that was rapidly going bald. Tom grinned when he saw the brand-new sports shirt that Chow was wearing. The chef liked flashy shirts, but this one was even louder and more hideous than usual, with large orange sunbursts on a green-and-purple background.

"Kinda like this little number, do you?" The ex-cowpoke chuckled proudly. "I picked it up fer a song through the latest mail-order catalog."

Preening himself like a peacock, he turned from side to side to show off the shirt from all angles. Tom squinted his eyes painfully and peered at the shirt through his fingers.

"You'll have to excuse me, Chow, but I can't make it out so well. I left my sunglasses home this morning."

Bud roared with laughter, but Chow took the ribbing in his usual good-natured fashion.

"You know what this hydrophobiated hoss thief

was tellin' me?" he remarked, jerking his thumb in Bud's direction.

"Sounded like something about a pair of boots," replied Tom cautiously.

"You figgerin' out somethin' special in that line?"

"Well, if we make this expedition to the South Pole that we're planning, we'll probably have to wear heated boots."

Chow gaped in astonishment. "Well, brand my radarscope!" Then he recovered and grinned a bit uncertainly. "Oh, I ketch on. A feller can't leave footprints on ice nohow!"

Tom laughed, then said, "Seriously, Chow, this trip will be quite an undertaking. You'd better start making a list of the food supplies you'll want to take along."

Bud winked. "To add to the stewed whale blubber and penguin soup you'll probably be serving us," he said. Bud was referring to Chow's well-known weakness for dreaming up exotic dishes of his own concoction.

"You jest leave all that to me, son," the cook said reassuringly. "I reckon I can figger out some tasty dishes even fer a place like the South Pole." He then inquired how the expedition would travel.

"We'll take the *Sky Queen*," Tom told him, referring to his first great invention, the three-decked Flying Lab. "And probably a couple of cargo planes.

So you'll have a good galley to cook in and plenty of room for groceries."

After Chow had left for the plant kitchen to prepare lunch for the boys, Tom went back to his work on the new earth blaster. Leaving the structural details for the time being, the young inventor turned his attention to some chemical experiments.

"What cooks, chum?" inquired Bud. "I mean, besides lunch."

Tom was now mixing several chemicals in a large flask.

"I'm trying to find a new plasticizer for asbestalon," he explained.

"A new which-icizer?"

"Plasticizer." Tom laughed. "That's something you put into plastics to make them tough and pliable."

"What's the matter with the one you have now?" Bud asked. "The plastic coating you slapped on the earth blaster seemed like pretty good insulation."

Tom shook his head. "It's all right for insulating the machine against the heat of the atomic pile inside. But think what would happen when we get down in those frigid temperatures at the South Pole!"

"Well, don't keep me in suspense," Bud pursued. "What *would* happen?"

"The asbestalon we have now would probably

turn brittle and crack in the extreme cold. So I'm trying to work out some new stuff that will be suitable for both high and low temperatures."

Bud watched in silence as Tom stirred the mixture, then added a drop from another container.

"What's that?" Bud demanded.

"Boron fluoride etherate."

"Come again?"

"I'm using it as a catalyst to make the chemical reaction come off. It plays no part in the reaction itself, but it sort of sparks things for the other ingredients. Gives them a chemical hotfoot, you might say."

"Doesn't look to me as if it's doing much good," Bud commented, peering at the flask.

"Get your head out of the way," Tom said, "and I'll try a little more."

Holding the bottle at arm's length, he poured a drop or two more into the reaction flask.

The contents began to bubble violently. An instant later the flask exploded with a loud bang that shook the whole laboratory!

## CHAPTER 5

## THE WHISPERED CLUE

IT WAS several seconds after the explosion before Tom, dazed and shaken, managed to pick himself off the floor.

His face stung and smarted. Groggily, the young inventor brushed one hand across his cheek. When he brought it away, it was streaked with blood.

Beside him, Bud was just struggling to his feet. "Roarin' rockets!" he gasped. "What hit me?"

"A slight overdose of boron fluoride etherate," Tom said ruefully. "Sorry, pal. I should have taken better precautions on that experiment."

At that moment Chow Winkler and Hank Sterling burst into the lab, accompanied by several plant workmen.

"Holy smoke!" Hank exclaimed. "What's going on in here?"

"The boy genius was just showing me how to use a catalyst to spark a chemical reaction," Bud said with a chuckle. "He showed me all right! Then the roof fell in!"

"You two young'uns all right?" Chow demanded anxiously.

"Still in one piece," said Tom. "But I guess we could do with a little cleaning up."

Instinctively both boys had flung up their hands and arms to protect their eyes when the flask exploded. Both had suffered slight cuts from the flying glass, and their clothing was splattered with the chemical mixture, but otherwise they were uninjured.

Damage to the laboratory was also slight. One shattered windowpane, plus some broken test tubes and other minor chemical equipment, seemed to be the only items which needed replacing.

After leaving orders to have the debris cleaned up, Tom accompanied Bud to the Swift Enterprises infirmary, where their cuts were treated by the company nurse. Then they adjourned to the spacious private office in the main building which Tom shared with his father.

Tom's half of the office contained a huge modern desk and a large workbench which slid in or out of the wall at the push of a button.

Displayed in the room were models of Tom's most

important inventions, hand tooled by Arvid Hanson, chief modelmaker of Swift Enterprises. Among them was a large, perfectly scaled model of the *Sky Queen,* a silver replica of Tom's rocket ship, the *Star Spear,* resting on three red fins with its nose pointing skyward, and a copy of his jetmarine, the *Sea Dart,* in blue plastic. The largest item in the collection was a model of Tom's giant robot.

Over a tasty lunch of soup and sandwiches, which Chow brought them, the boys talked about Tom's experiment.

"What happens now?" Bud inquired. "You going to give up on that asbestalon?"

Tom shook his head. "Not yet. But in the next experiment I'll use a milder catalyst and take a few more precautions."

After lunch they returned to the laboratory. This time, Tom prepared to carry out the test behind a safety shield. He also suspended the flask over a quench tank into which he could plunge the chemical mixture in case the reaction showed signs of getting out of hand.

"You sure this new stuff is milder?" Bud grinned. "Or should I start diving out the window right now?"

"It's definitely milder," Tom reassured him. "It's titanium tetrachloride."

Using long-handled tongs, Tom reached past the

safety shield and poured a drop or two of the catalyst into the flask. Gradually the chemical mixture began to seethe and bubble.

"Looks as if it's working out all right," commented Bud. "But it sure smells terrible!"

Tom waited until he was certain the reaction was completed. Then he poured out the contents of the flask, allowed it to cool until it was a rubbery mass, and then proceeded to test the substance in several different ways.

Bud looked on with keen interest. "Well?" he asked finally.

The young inventor's face wore a pleased smile. "Bud, I believe this new form of asbestalon is all I hoped for and a lot more besides!"

Bud shook his head admiringly. "Chum, I've got to hand it to you. I don't know how you do it, but you always come through with the goods!"

Tom added, "Of course we'll have to run some more tests on it in the cold lab to make sure it'll stand up under sub-zero temperatures. Then, if it works out okay, we can have the chemical division start making it up in quantity."

The door opened and Harlan Ames strode into the room. "Big news!" he exclaimed.

"What's up?" Tom asked the security chief.

"I think they've nailed those two thugs working with Bronich—the ones who tied you up! The State

Police caught two men today who answer the description! Captain Rock wants you to identify them."

"Now we're getting somewhere!" Bud exclaimed. "Let's go."

Fifteen minutes later Police Captain Rock greeted them in his office. "Sit down and I'll have the men brought in."

Their wrists handcuffed, the two men entered the room with a husky state trooper as guard.

"How about it, Tom?" said Captain Rock. "Are these the men?"

Tom got up from his chair and went over to study the prisoners closely.

"No doubt about it," he announced. "I can identify this fellow by the small scar over his left eyebrow. And the other one was wearing the same belt he has on now." The belt was unmistakable. It had a large fancy buckle studded with colored stones.

"All right, Bank, and you too, Dutt," Captain Rock said. "Start talking. And you'd better make it as convincing as your police records!"

"We got nothin' to say," mumbled Bank, the one with the scar.

"Oh, no?" Bud clenched his fists. "Maybe you two would like the same kind of a going-over you gave my pal!"

"Take it easy, Bud," Tom said quietly, putting a

restraining hand on his friend's shoulder. "It's true they tied me, but they didn't try to rough me up."

The prisoners shot him a grateful glance as the young inventor continued speaking.

"Look," he said, "there's no sense in taking the rap for someone else. I'm fairly sure the whole thing wasn't your idea, anyhow. So why not tell us who put you up to it?"

"Why should we!"

"Because that gunman who stole part of my invention is a foreign agent. If you want to cover up for him, you may both end up in prison on charges of treason and espionage!"

Captain Rock pounded his desk. "Right, and by the time you birds get out you'll have whiskers down to your knees!"

The prisoners looked at each other apprehensively, then back at Tom and Captain Rock.

"Okay, you win," growled Bank. "What do you want to know?"

"Who hired you?" asked Tom.

"The guy you were just talkin' about. The one who swiped your truck."

"Where can we find him?"

The man shrugged. "Search me. He wouldn't even tell us his name."

Bank paused and shifted his weight uncomfortably. Dutt stared at the floor.

"Come on, speak up!" snapped Captain Rock. "We haven't got all day!"

"Well, there is one thing I can tell you," Bank said. "I heard him gabbin' on the phone once. He said he figured on stickin' around till he got the blueprints and specifications."

"Whom was he talking to?" asked Ames.

"Don't ask me. Most of the time he was jabberin' away in some foreign lingo I couldn't understand."

"That's all you can tell us?" pressed Captain Rock.

"That's all we know."

"Okay, take them back to their cells," the police chief said to the guard.

Just before they were escorted out, Dutt turned to Tom. "Go to 95 Western Drive," he said tersely.

"What's there?"

"You'll find out," Dutt said. "That's all I can tell you."

As soon as the prisoners were led away, Captain Rock ordered two of his men to Western Drive.

"Wait a minute, Captain," Tom said. "Two uniformed police in a squad car might tip off the man we want. Let me take Barclay and Ames to scout the place. We'll report back to you."

The captain agreed.

Western Drive was a broad, spacious thoroughfare that wound along the shore of Lake Carlopa.

"Boy, I'd sure like to go out today in that new

sailboat of Sandy's!" Bud remarked, gazing at the blue, sparkling waters as they drove along.

Harlan Ames was watching the numbers of the houses and apartment buildings. Suddenly he exclaimed, "Look! There's the place!"

As Tom swerved to the curb and applied the brakes, both boys gave a gasp of astonishment. The building which bore the address of 95 Western Drive was the Excelsis Club, a favorite haunt of wealthy sportsmen! Its front faced the street and the rear of the property backed onto the lake shore.

"Now what would Bronich be doing in a place like this?" Bud exclaimed. "I thought that prisoner was giving us a bum steer!"

"Let's inquire inside," Tom said. "At least we can find out if anyone knows him."

As they were getting out of the jeep, a man emerged from a cluster of cars in the club's private parking lot and headed toward a side door of the building. Just before entering, he turned his head for a glance at the newcomers, and Tom caught a brief glimpse of his face.

"That's Bronich!" cried Tom, and made a dash for the side entrance. Bud and Ames followed.

The heavy door, marked PRIVATE, had already slammed shut by the time they reached it. Tom and his friends pounded on it loudly and rattled the handle but got no response.

The three hurried back around the corner of the building and ran up the flagged walk.

Under a striped awning, a towering doorman in a gold-braided uniform stood guard at the entrance. As Ames and the boys tried to rush past him, he stuck out his right arm to bar the way.

"May I see your cards, please?"

"Hang it all," Ames said impatiently. "We have no cards, but we're here on very important business!"

The doorman assumed a frozen, supercilious expression.

"Sorry, sir," he replied firmly, "but my orders are to admit no one to the Excelsis Club except regular members!"

# CHAPTER 6

# BRONICH VANISHES

FUMING WITH IMPATIENCE, Harlan Ames told the doorman who he and the boys were, and demanded to see the manager.

"He's not available," the man said icily.

"We're trailing someone who's wanted by the police!" Tom explained. "He's a dangerous foreign agent and we saw him enter this club through the side door!"

"Sorry, sir, but I have my orders."

At a nod from Tom, Bud and Ames followed the young inventor in a search of some other means of entrance to the club.

"That frozen-faced doorman!" raged Bud, as they circled the building. "We should've grabbed him by the seat of the pants and tossed him in the lake!"

"Never mind him," Tom said. "The important

thing right now is to make sure Bronich doesn't get away!"

At the back of the building a door was standing slightly open. From inside came a clatter of dishes, and an appetizing smell of food wafted out through a whirring ventilator.

"Must be the club kitchen," Bud said. "That's as good a way in as any other!"

Before Tom or Ames could stop him, he went charging inside.

The clatter of dishes stopped for a moment. Then there was an angry babble of voices.

A moment later Bud came hurtling out of the kitchen door to land sprawling at the feet of his two companions!

In the doorway stood a huge, olive-skinned, mustachioed man in a chef's cap. As he poured out a flood of voluble Italian, he waved a rolling pin angrily at Bud.

"Next'a time, I won't'a be so gentle!" he finished threateningly. "And you can tell'a that to you'a friends, too!"

"Whew!" Bud said, as he picked himself up and dusted off his slacks. "That guy belongs on a pro football team! What a blocker he'd make!"

"Looks as if we're out of luck," said Tom, trying hard not to laugh at Bud's discomfiture.

"No use wasting any more time," Ames suggested.

"I'll put in a call to the State Police. While I'm gone, you two stay here and keep a sharp lookout for Bronich, in case he tries to leave!"

Nobody had emerged from the building by the time Ames returned, and two minutes later the trio saw a police car speed up the street. As it stopped in front of the club, the car doors opened and three state troopers stepped out, led by Captain Rock. Turning to his men, he said crisply:

"Foster, you take the side door! Let no one leave! Jorgens, you and Brant guard the back!"

At sight of the police the doorman's eyes bugged out and his jaw dropped. This time, he opened the door promptly, and Captain Rock entered, followed by Tom, Ames, and Bud.

Inside, the club secretary came hurrying forward to greet them. He was a bony, hawk-nosed man wearing pince-nez glasses. Tom told him why they were there.

"The whole charge is ridiculous!" he snorted in a nasal, high-pitched voice when told that a foreign spy had been seen entering the club.

"Mind if we look for ourselves?" Captain Rock said grimly.

From the secretary's expression, it was clear that he did mind. But when the police captain produced a warrant, there was nothing he could do but stand aside.

Assisted by Harlan Ames and the boys, the police searched the club from top to bottom, but they found not the slightest trace of Bronich!

"Well, I'll be a boiled bazooka!" said Bud, scratching his head in puzzlement. "We know dog-gone well Bronich came in here. We saw him with our own eyes!"

"Well, he's not here now," said Captain Rock, "so it looks as if he flew the coop."

"But how could he?" argued Tom. "We were watching the place all the time!"

The police captain shrugged. "If he knew you fellows had spotted him, he may have sneaked out in disguise—maybe a chauffeur's uniform."

After the troopers had left, Ames was still angry and dissatisfied. But he said nothing until he and the boys had driven away in the jeep.

Then, a short distance from the club, he asked Tom to pull over to the curb.

"What's wrong?" Bud asked.

"I have a hunch Bronich is still hiding out at the Excelsis Club."

The security chief climbed out of the jeep.

"I'm going back to do some more investigating," he went on. "I'll keep out of sight and see what I can learn. If Bronich thinks we've gone, maybe he'll give himself away!"

Tom and Bud drove back to Swift Enterprises. It

was almost closing time when they entered the gates of the sprawling experimental station.

In the main building, Miss Trent, the Swifts' capable and efficient secretary, told Tom, "Your father just got back from Washington. He'd like to see you at once!"

Tom hurried to their private office.

"That was a quick flight, Dad!" he exclaimed, in response to his father's greeting.

"Tom, I have great news!" announced Mr. Swift. "That's why I flew back to Shopton immediately. The government officials I talked to are very much interested in your proposed expedition to the South Pole."

"Have they given us the go-ahead?"

"They have, indeed; even granted permission for us to explore any part of the Antarctic claimed by the United States. And Uncle Sam will also lend us funds to help finance the expedition, provided we take along several government scientists!"

Tom gave a whoop of delight and pumped his father's arm up and down in a handshake of joyful enthusiasm.

"Dad, that's wonderful! Let's start planning for the trip right now!"

Mr. Swift smiled at his son's excitement. He fully shared Tom's reaction to the promise of high adventure. But he added a note of caution.

"Don't forget this will be a tremendous undertaking. And it all depends on your perfecting the new model of your atomic earth blaster!"

Then he pressed the switch of his intercom. "Miss Trent, please phone Mr. Newton at the Swift Construction Company. Ask him to come to my office for a very important meeting as soon as possible!"

While they waited for Uncle Ned, Tom told his father about the latest developments in the case of Bronich and the two hired thugs. He also described the progress he had made on the new blaster, including his invention of a new form of asbestalon for use at low temperatures.

"Great work, son!" Mr. Swift congratulated him. "At this rate, your new blaster may be ready even sooner than we'd expected."

Shortly after that, Uncle Ned arrived at Swift Enterprises, carrying a bulging brief case. After greeting him, Tom asked for permission to let Bud Barclay sit in on the meeting.

Both men readily agreed, and Bud was sent for immediately. When he arrived, all four pulled up chairs around a highly polished mahogany table and got down to business.

First, Mr. Swift gave a detailed report of the news from Washington. Bud was as wildly enthusiastic as Tom had been. But Uncle Ned reserved judgment until he had time to study the details.

The expedition was discussed from all angles. Tom frankly pointed out the hazards they would be facing. Uncle Ned drew up a rough estimate of the total cost. Even with government financial backing for the expedition, it would amount to a staggering sum!

Uncle Ned and Mr. Swift faced each other soberly across the table. The risk was tremendous. But finally they came to a decision. They agreed to undertake the South Pole expedition, with the investment of large sums of money from both the Swift Construction Company and Swift Enterprises!

"It's only fair to warn you, Tom," Uncle Ned added, "that we're staking everything on the hope of success. If your project fails, our firms will be ruined!"

Tom's heart pounded, but he managed to reply calmly, "I'll do my best to make sure the expedition succeeds, Uncle Ned!"

Tom realized that success of his venture would necessarily mean the loss of the blaster, which would disintegrate upon striking the earth's molten core. But this loss would be only a fraction of the value of the endless source of pure iron obtained!

Bud brought up the question of clothing. "I suppose we'll all have to go around in fur parkas down there," he remarked.

"We'll need more than fur suits," Tom replied.

"Any clothing we wear will have to be radiation-proof."

Bud frowned in disbelief and asked, "Won't the atomic pile inside your blaster be sheathed in Tomasite?" He referred to the amazing new plastic invented by Mr. Swift, which, although very light in weight, absorbed gamma rays more effectively than either lead or concrete. Mrs. Swift had named it in honor of both father and son.

"Sure," Tom replied, "but suppose we have to tear down the machine for repairs. And don't forget that the dirt and rock will be converted into gas by atomic energy inside the blaster. Consequently the fumes rising up to the surface will be slightly radioactive, too."

Mr. Swift offered a suggestion. "I think the answer to that problem is to have your clothing impregnated with Tomasite," he said.

A rapping of knuckles sounded on the office door. In answer to Mr. Swift's "Come in!" Chow Winkler waddled into the room, pushing a lunch cart loaded with steaming dishes of food. The Texan grinned.

"Seein' as how you gents are prob'ly gonna be late fer supper at home," he explained, "I figgered I'd better rustle you up some grub right here."

With a shock of surprise, the four conferees saw that they had been talking much longer than they realized. It was almost half past seven. Outside, daylight had faded into dusk.

"This South Pole trip will be quite a change from Texas, Chow," Uncle Ned remarked with a smile, as they all consumed the food hungrily.

"How d'you mean?"

"All the ice and snow you'll have to contend with." He turned to Tom. "How cold does it get down there, anyhow?"

"It gets *mighty* cold," replied the young inventor. "Some places the temperature never rises above five degrees even in midsummer. And in winter, it drops down to a hundred below zero!"

"Leapin' cactus!" Beneath his heavy tan Chow's face paled, and he gave a nervous shudder. "Why, man alive, that's worse'n a blizzard on the open plains! Brand my jets, I ain't so sure I wanta go 'long on this ole expedition!"

"Don't worry, Chow." Tom grinned. "We'll have electrical heating units built into our suits, with thermostats to regulate the temperature. All you'll have to do is set the right temperature on the dial and you can stay as warm as you like, no matter how cold it gets outside!"

The Texan chuckled with relief. "Now you're talkin', boy!" But then his face became sober again. "Come to think of it, that means I'll have to do all my cookin' with gloves on—an' that's somethin' no self-respectin' chuck-wagon cook would be caught dead with!"

The phone jangled shrilly.

Tom answered it. "Hello? . . . Oh, hi! . . . Yes, we're still here at the plant. My dad just got back from Washington. . . . What! . . . All right, fine! You stay there, and Bud and I will be right over to join you!"

As he put down the phone, his father flashed a quizzical glance.

"That was Harlan Ames," Tom explained. "He thinks he's found a secret exit from the Excelsis Club, and wants Bud and me to join him right away!"

Five minutes later the boys were speeding off in Bud's red convertible.

Ames had arranged to meet them on the shore line of Lake Carlopa, just off Western Drive, a short distance from the Excelsis Club.

When they reached the meeting place, Bud turned the car off onto the grassy strip that ran between the paved roadway and the concrete embankment.

It was now completely dark, but at a shrill whistle from Tom, a light flashed from the water's edge—Ames' signal.

The boys clambered over the edge of the embankment and dropped into the waiting boat.

"I figured a rowboat would be safer than a motorboat," Ames explained. "Quieter that way. I've greased the oarlocks, too."

Tom took the rower's seat and Ames shoved off from the concrete wall. As they headed toward the Excelsis Club, a rising moon cast a silvery glow across the waters of the lake.

"Just where is this secret exit you found?" Tom asked.

"Wait till I show you," said Ames. "If I'm right, it'll explain how Bronich made his getaway without being seen!"

A few minutes later the security chief whispered to Tom, "Pull in here!"

The windows of the Excelsis Club were aglow with light, but the shore line was shrouded in darkness. Ames snapped on his flashlight and played the beam along the embankment. Suddenly he held the beam steady, and Tom gave a stifled gasp of surprise. Partly overgrown by vines and creepers, yet clearly revealed by the glow of the flashlight, was an opening in the concrete! Four feet above the water line a narrow flight of stone steps led upward.

"Let's take a look inside," Tom said excitedly, guiding the craft toward the opening.

"Better not leave the boat here," Ames cautioned. "It might give us away."

Tom readily agreed, and Bud added, "I noticed some boat rings a little way beyond here. We can tie up to one and then come back here."

After tying up the boat, they crept back along

the top of the embankment, crouching low to avoid being seen. When they reached the stone steps, they descended cautiously.

Once again, Ames snapped on his flashlight. Five steps led downward, then the dank stone passageway leveled off for twenty feet. At the end of this, another flight of stone steps led upward.

"Come on!" Tom urged.

Softly they made their way up the slippery, moss-grown steps. The stairway ended at a trap door above their heads. From the other side of it came a clatter of dishes and the sound of voices.

"The club kitchen!" Ames whispered. "Right over us!"

"From the looks of things, the club could be a cover-up for a group of foreign agents," remarked Tom, "especially with this passageway in and out of the place. A perfect setup for espionage and sabotage agents!"

"With Swift Enterprises as their target!" Bud added.

Suddenly Ames switched off the flashlight, plunging them into darkness.

"Listen!" he hissed. "Someone's coming!"

Bud tensed. "And there's no place to hide!"

# CHAPTER 7

# A BOLD OFFER

THE NOISE they had heard was that of a boat bumping against the concrete wall near the entrance to the passageway. Judging from the sounds that followed, whoever was aboard was now debarking.

Tom reached out and grabbed Ames and Bud by the arm.

"Listen!" he whispered. "Just before the light went out, I noticed a recess in the left-hand side of the passage. Let's see if it's big enough to hide in!"

Quickly turning to the left, they began groping blindly.

"Here it is!" Tom exclaimed softly. The other two joined him in squeezing into the narrow space.

They could hear footsteps now, coming up the stairway. Holding their breath, the three friends flattened themselves against the wall.

The newcomer was a man. He was carrying a flashlight, but fortunately he aimed it downward at the steps to avoid stumbling. Without seeing Tom and his companions, he reached for the trap door.

Tom gave a faint sigh of relief as the man rapped on it several times. A moment later it opened, and a ray of light penetrated the darkness. A voice said, "Oh, it's you, Podski."

The newcomer asked, "Is Bronich here?"

"No. He phoned to say that he's not coming tonight. He has some business to attend to—about Tom Swift."

Tom leaned out of his hiding place to get a view of the speakers. It was impossible to see the person in the kitchen. But in the glow of light, Tom clearly saw the man who had come through the passageway. He was a short, heavy-set individual, partly bald. Tom had never seen him before.

There were a few more remarks in low tones which Tom could not hear. Then the man called Podski climbed up into the kitchen, and the trap door closed behind him.

The trio emerged from their hiding place and consulted on what to do next.

"If we trail this fellow Podski," Ames said, "he may lead us to other members of the gang. Perhaps even to Bronich himself!"

"If we don't want to lose him, we'd better split

up and watch every entrance to the club," Tom said.

"Good idea," agreed the security chief. "Suppose I take the front door. Tom, you watch at the side. Bud, you keep an eye on this exit."

The boys agreed to Ames' plan and they took up their posts. Tom crouched in a thick mass of shrubbery where he could have a clear view of the side door without being seen.

Time went by slowly. Tom felt painfully stiff and cramped. Again and again he shifted position to ease the strain on his aching muscles.

Finally the club guests began going home. Cars were driven away from the private parking lot. All the lights were turned off inside the building as the last employee left. A short time later Ames rejoined Tom.

"Any sign of Podski?" he asked.

When the young inventor said no, they made their way back to the shore line, where Bud was standing watch. He, too, had seen no sign of their quarry, and Podski's boat was still tied up.

"What happened to that guy?" Bud said impatiently.

"That's what I'd like to know," grumbled the security chief. "Unless he's still in there somewhere."

Tom had a sudden idea. "Let's try that trap door. Maybe it's not locked!"

*The trap door opened freely in response to Tom's push*

Eagerly they scrambled up to the opening in the concrete ceiling. The trap door opened freely in response to Tom's push!

Silently they climbed into the kitchen. The room was shrouded in darkness. Ames snapped on his flashlight and played it around. Its beam revealed glistening white tile walls, cooking implements, three cookstoves, two long wooden tables, and numerous racks of dishes and silverware.

There certainly was no place for anyone to hide.

"Come on," Tom whispered. "Let's try the other rooms."

One by one, they searched every room in the building. But there was no trace of Podski or anyone else. He had vanished as completely as Bronich had.

"He must have left by the front or side door just before we started watching," Tom said.

Bud groaned. "You mean all this guard duty tonight was a waste of time?"

Tom shrugged. "Can't be helped. I guess the only thing we can do now is notify the police."

Using one of the club telephones, Ames called the State Police barracks and left a message for Captain Rock, telling him everything that had happened. Then the three friends returned by boat to the spot where the red convertible was parked, and drove home.

Next morning, Tom continued to work on his

new blaster. Quickly he mapped out the details for the built-in cooling system.

Next, he picked up the telephone and dialed one of the inside numbers at Swift Enterprises.

"Have the tractor truck with the experimental blaster driven around to my lab, please," he ordered.

When the truck arrived, Tom began making blueprints for the new blaster. From time to time, he would refer to the experimental model or remove one of the inner parts for close inspection and testing.

After a hasty lunch, the young inventor put in a call to Uncle Ned Newton at the Swift Construction Company.

"What's up, Tom?"

"Uncle Ned, how soon can you start building my new blaster at the construction plant?"

"Do you have any working drawings for us?"

"Yes, the design is pretty well jelled. I can send over the drawings later this afternoon and meet with your engineers tomorrow."

"Fast work, Tom! Glad to hear it. I'll assign a team for the project immediately. By the way, what kind of steel will you need?"

"The best. I'll need a high-strength alloy that will stand up at high temperatures and have strong resistance to corrosive gases."

"All right," Uncle Ned replied. "I have a batch of chrome-nickel-moly that should fill the bill. And we'll look for those drawings before quitting time today!"

In midafternoon, as Tom was finishing the last of his sketches, Chow Winkler dropped in to discuss food supplies needed for the South Pole expedition.

"That sure is a mean-lookin' contraption you got parked outside!" the cook added. "Is that what you're diggin' through to China with?"

"Not exactly." Tom grinned. "That's only my experimental model. The blaster we take down to the South Pole will be somewhat different."

"How different?"

"Well, look at these drawings. Instead of those digging devices you see sticking out of the front end of our experimental model, the new one will have four electrodes spaced around the nose and a long guide vane sticking right out of the center."

"What's the idea o' them things?" Chow asked.

"Well, you see, the old model just ground up the dirt and rocks mechanically. But on my new blaster, these electrodes sticking out in front will melt any rock on contact. Then the molten liquid will be drawn in through these intake ports, and further smelting will take place inside the machine. The resulting hot gases will jet out through these exhaust ports at the rear."

The ex-cowpoke swallowed hard and scratched his head.

"Well, I reckon it's okay if you say so, son," he

commented, "but it jest looks like some kind o' giant bug to me. An' it sure ain't the kind anyone in Texas would want to see crawlin' around out on the range!"

Tom burst out laughing.

"You're gonna test this contraption before we get down to that land o' ice 'n' snow, ain't you?" the cook went on anxiously.

"I'll tell you a secret, Chow," the young inventor replied. "I'm going to offer to dig that tunnel through Pine Hill for the extra water supply Shopton needs. Come to think of it, I may as well do that right now."

Snatching up the phone, Tom first called his father for approval. Obtaining it, he called the water company and asked to speak to Mr. Greenup.

"Well, what is it now?" growled the president.

"Mr. Greenup, you spoke about tunneling through Pine Hill to tap an extra supply of water from Silver Lake."

"What about it?"

"I'm willing to undertake that job for you," said Tom. "And what's more, I'll do it absolutely free."

"What!" Greenup sounded flabbergasted. Then he added suspiciously, "I presume there are some strings attached to your offer?"

"None at all," Tom replied. "It'll give me a chance to put my earth blaster through a real workout and at the same time benefit the whole community."

Greenup was silent for a moment.

"That's a mighty generous offer," he said finally. "But of course I'll have to take it up with the Water Committee of the Town Council before I give you a definite answer. Suppose I call you tomorrow morning."

The next day Tom waited eagerly for a reply. Shortly before noon, Greenup phoned to say that the committee had voted to accept his offer with thanks.

Tom was jubilant. After lunch he drove to the construction company plant where he conferred with the engineers about building the new blaster. Later, he stopped at Uncle Ned's office to tell him about the Pine Hill project.

"Do you think that will be safe, in view of the radioactive exhaust gases?" Mr. Newton asked.

"I won't use our South Pole blaster to dig the tunnel," replied Tom. "I intend to build a special model for this job. It will utilize most of my new design features and give me a chance to test them out. But instead of using the electric smelting principle to convert the rock into gases, this machine will operate on a mechanical grinding principle, just like my first model."

Uncle Ned considered for a few moments.

"Okay," he agreed. "The job may help you iron out any bugs in your new design, and perhaps suggest other improvements. But no chrome-nickel-moly for this model. That stuff's too expensive! You'll have to build the machine with regular mild-carbon steel."

Late that afternoon Tom was in his private laboratory at Swift Enterprises with Bud Barclay. Work was over for the day, and the two boys were discussing the expedition to the Antarctic.

Suddenly an alarm bell clanged.

"The radarscope!" Bud exclaimed. "Wait'll I switch on the set!"

The two boys tensely watched the scope. As the scanner swept around the screen, a blip of light showed up in the five-o'clock sector, then began moving slowly in toward the center.

"Must be some kind of aircraft," remarked Bud. "But what the dickens is the pilot up to?"

"We'll soon find out!" said Tom. "Let's go."

Dashing outside, the boys stared skyward to the southeast.

"There it is!" Tom shouted.

A helicopter was spiraling crazily down!

**CHAPTER 8**

# A THREAT OF REVENGE

THE HELICOPTER was yawing wildly from side to side as it floated downward.

"That pilot must be balmy!" Bud exclaimed.

"Maybe he's hurt," said Tom.

The two boys watched in puzzled and anxious concern, realizing they were helpless to aid the stricken craft.

"Let's try for a closer look!" Tom cried. He ran back to the laboratory and returned a moment later with a pair of field glasses.

"Can you make anything out?" asked Bud, as his friend trained the glasses skyward.

"Looks as if something *is* wrong with the pilot," Tom replied, "but it's hard to tell for sure from this angle."

As soon as they could judge the approximate spot

where the ship would land, the boys leaped into a jeep and speeded toward it.

Just as they reached the scene, the helicopter hit the ground with a jarring impact that almost buckled one of the landing-gear struts. In the the cabin was a single occupant, slumped over the controls.

A crash truck already had reached the spot. As the boys rushed to offer assistance, plants guards and other employees came running from all directions.

"Is he hurt badly?" Tom asked, as the crash crew lifted the pilot's limp body out of the cabin.

*As they reached the scene, the helicopter*

"Doesn't seem to be hurt at all," replied one of the men. "Maybe the jolt knocked him cold."

By the time he was carried into the plant infirmary on a stretcher, the pilot showed signs of reviving. As they laid him on a cot, his eyes fluttered open.

He was a pale-faced, slightly built man in his early twenties. Tom did not recognize him as any local flier of his acquaintance.

After examining the pilot, the company doctor

*hit the ground with a jarring impact*

announced that he had suffered no broken bones or other injuries.

"What happened?" Tom asked the airman. "You gave us quite a scare."

"Sorry," he replied shakily. "I guess I must have blacked out at the controls. I—I was just flying along and next thing I knew they were carrying me in here on a stretcher."

"What is your name?"

"Landis—Jerry Landis." The man started to get up. "Well, I—I may as well be on my way."

The doctor suggested that he rest for a while. "Since you blacked out once this afternoon, I certainly wouldn't advise going up again so soon— especially when you have no copilot."

But Landis refused to remain in the infirmary. "I'll leave the copter here, if you don't mind, and send for it tomorrow morning," he said to Tom. Turning to the doctor, he added, "If you'll have the nurse call a taxi for me, I won't trouble you any further." A few minutes later Landis rode off.

Early the next morning Tom and Bud drove out to Pine Hill to look over the site of the proposed digging operations. A crew of surveyors already was busy, lining up the route that the tunnel would follow to Silver Lake.

"Looks as if you've got quite a job on your hands, chum!" Bud said.

"It'll probably mean plenty of headaches," agreed Tom, "but think what an experience it'll be! I can hardly wait to get started!"

Suddenly a loud, angry voice burst out:

"Which one of you two is Tom Swift?"

Startled, the boys turned to look at the speaker, who had come up behind them. He was a burly, red-faced individual in a rumpled tan suit and a Panama hat. A half-chewed cigar protruded from one corner of his mouth.

"Well, speak up! I asked which one of you cubs is Tom Swift?"

"I'm Tom Swift," the inventor replied coolly. "What can I do for you?"

"Do for me?" roared the stranger. "You've done enough as it is, you meddling young fool! Is it true you've offered to drive that tunnel through Pine Hill for nothing?"

"That's right."

The stranger's eyes narrowed and he shook a ham-like fist in Tom's face. "By thunder, I oughta whale the tar out of you right here and now!"

Bud Barclay's jaw jutted out in a surge of anger at the man's hectoring manner and insulting words.

"Watch where you wave that fist of yours, mister," he said, "or someone may shove it down your throat —and it might just be me!"

From the way he stepped forward and doubled up his fists, it was clear that Bud meant business. With his husky shoulders and muscular arms he was more than a match for the blustering stranger, but Tom quickly interposed.

"I'll handle this, Bud." Turning to the stranger, he said, "Just who are you?"

"Picken—that's who I am! Charles Picken, head of the Picken Engineering Company. We had this tunnel job all wrapped up before you came along, and now you've cheated us out of a half-million-dollar contract!"

"Tom Swift never cheated you or anyone else out of anything!" declared Bud angrily. "The Water Committee was mighty grateful for Tom's offer, and so is every other civic-minded person in this town!"

Tom said quietly, "I have my own reasons for taking on this project. Besides, Shopton needs water badly, and I'm quite sure I can drive this tunnel much faster than you could possibly handle the job."

"That's what you think!" Picken sneered. "But I'll see to it that you never do complete this tunnel! Take it from me, you're in for trouble!" He turned away and strode down the hill.

"Tom, that guy is spoiling for a fight," muttered Bud. "I still think we should have settled this right here and now. He was certainly asking for it!"

"That wouldn't solve anything, Bud. Let him go."

Nevertheless, when they returned to Swift Enterprises later that morning, Bud made it a point to report the threat to Harlan Ames.

"I've heard of Picken," said the security chief. "He has a bad reputation all over the state for using unscrupulous tactics against business competitors. We'll keep an eye on him!"

In his private laboratory, Tom continued work on the South Pole blaster. A new idea had occurred to him for improving the efficiency of the power converter. This was the equipment which harnessed the energy of the atomic pile to smelt and vaporize the rocky ore.

Using a slide rule, Tom quickly worked out a number of equations. His mental calculations had been right. By changing gear ratios in the power-conversion equipment, he should be able to make the blaster operate at anywhere from twenty-five to fifty percent higher speeds than he had first planned.

He decided to make the necessary changes in the blueprints at once. Getting up from his lab stool, Tom went to the shelf where he had left his copies of the drawings, but they were not there.

"Guess I must have locked them in the cabinet last night," he decided.

With his electronic key, he beamed open the lock of the cabinet and riffled through the contents. The blueprints were not there, either.

Quickly he went to the phone and dialed Bud at the underground hangar.

"Bud, do you recall seeing the blueprints for the South Pole blaster when you came to my lab this morning, just before we went out to Pine Hill?"

"No, I don't think so," replied Bud slowly. "Why? Is anything wrong?"

"I hope not," Tom said in a worried voice. "But I seem to have mislaid them."

"I'll come over and help you hunt," his chum offered.

"Okay," Tom replied, and after hanging up, searched all the shelves but did not find the blueprints.

Next, he telephoned Miss Trent.

"I can't find the blueprints for the new South Pole blaster," he explained. "Please look in the office and see if you can find them in my desk or any of the file cabinets. Try Dad's desk, too."

"Do you want to hold on while I look?" asked the secretary.

"No, take your time and search carefully. If you find the drawings, call me right back."

Without waiting for her report, he contacted the maintenance department and talked to the janitor who had cleaned up his office the night before. But the janitor, too, had no recollection of having seen the blueprints.

Just as Tom was hanging up the phone, Bud walked into the lab.

"Any luck?" he inquired.

"Not so far."

Anxiously the two boys proceeded to give every drawer and storage compartment in the lab a thorough going-over. But they had found no trace of the blueprints by the time Miss Trent called back to report that her search had been a vain one.

As he put the phone down, Tom turned to his friend with a grim expression.

"Bud, I'm afraid those plans have been stolen!"

**CHAPTER 9**

# PURSUIT ON THE LAKE

TOM AND BUD faced each other in dismayed silence. Tom was the first to speak.

"We'd better report the theft of the blueprints to Harlan Ames pronto!"

"Right!"

Five minutes later the boys entered Ames' office in the security building. The chief listened gravely to Tom's story about the theft of the plans.

"Any idea who might have taken them?" he asked.

"Lots of ideas but no proof."

"Well, how many people had an opportunity to steal them?"

Before Tom could reply, Bud Barclay snapped his fingers.

"I'll bet I know who's back of this! That bull-headed contractor we tangled with this morning—Charles Picken!"

Tom disagreed. "I doubt that Picken is responsible," he said. "If the thief is an outsider, he must have worn a gadget similar to our electronic amulets to avoid being detected by the radarscope. Only a well-trained scientist could devise such a thing."

"In other words, someone like Bronich—or maybe Podski," put in Ames.

Tom nodded gloomily.

The electronic amulets were devices worn in the form of a bracelet by all workmen and visitors who had business inside the grounds of Swift Enterprises. The purpose was to trap radar impulses and thus keep the reflections from showing up as blips of light on the radar screen.

"I may be wrong," went on Tom, "but I have a hunch the thief was a stowaway in that copter."

"Too late to check up now," said Ames. "Landis called for his ship early this morning and flew it away personally."

Tom drove his right fist angrily into the palm of his left hand. "What a fool I was not to suspect him right from the first! It was a perfect setup!"

"You mean he was only faking unconsciousness?" asked Bud.

"Of course. The thief probably remained hidden inside the copter till we took Landis to the infirmary. Then he sneaked out and grabbed the blueprints while the door to my lab was standing open. After that, all he had to do was lie low and wait for Landis to fly him out again this morning!"

"Sounds as if you've hit the nail right on the head, chum," agreed Bud. "Which means our job now is to find Landis."

"If he has a pilot's license, we may be able to trace him through the CAA," said Ames. "I'll give them a call right now."

While Ames was talking to the Civil Aeronautics Administration, the two boys returned to Tom's laboratory, where Chow Winkler served them lunch. Shortly after two o'clock, Ames called back.

Jerry Landis, he reported, was a licensed helicopter pilot. His credentials were all in order, although his present address was unknown. The police had been alerted to watch out for him, but so far neither Landis nor his helicopter had been found.

"Here's something else that may interest you," concluded Ames. "Our friend Landis is also a member of the Excelsis Club!"

Just as Tom was passing the news along to Bud, Sandy and her friend Phyllis Newton walked into the laboratory. Phyllis, a pretty girl with long dark hair and laughing brown eyes, was the daughter of Uncle Ned Newton.

"Well, are you two all set to go?" asked Sandy gaily.

"Go where?" said Bud.

"Why, Tom, didn't you tell him?" Sandy turned to her brother with a puzzled frown.

"Gosh, Sandy, I've been so busy that it slipped my mind!"

Bud looked from brother to sister. "Well, don't keep it a secret. What's this all about?"

"Sandy cooked up a double date for us," explained Tom. "We were all supposed to go sailing on the lake this afternoon in the *Mary Nestor*."

The *Mary Nestor* was Sandy's sleek new sailboat, named in honor of Mrs. Swift.

"I want to try it out for speed," she said, turning to Bud. "You see, the final yacht club race of the season is next Saturday, and this'll be my last chance for a trial run before the race."

"Wonderful!" Bud exclaimed. "What are we waiting for? Let's go!"

The dark-haired young flier, whose parents lived in San Francisco, loved all forms of outdoor sports but was especially fond of sailing.

Tom, however, held back. "I'm sorry, gang, but I have a million things to do! I'm afraid I'll have to beg off this time."

The girls let out a wail of protest.

"Tom, you can't let us down like this, after Phyl and I have been counting on you!" Sandy protested. She hastily pulled a copy of the racing announcement out of her shoulder bag and added:

"Just look at all the people who've signed up for the race! We won't stand a chance against competition like that unless you figure out the angles for us!"

At that moment Tom whistled sharply. He had been idly scanning the entry list.

"Bud! Look!"

"What's the matter?"

"Landis—Jerry Landis! His name is down here on the list of entrants!"

Bud bent over Tom's shoulder to see for himself. "Well, I'll be a jumpin' jet jockey!"

In reply to the girls' puzzled queries, Tom told them about Landis' helicopter descent and the subsequent theft of the blaster plans.

"If this Mr. Landis was in on the crime, you certainly should come with us," said Phyl. "You might find him sailing on the lake."

"Hey, that's an idea!" exclaimed Bud.

"Smart girl, Phyl." Tom smiled admiringly. "Okay, you've sold me. Let's go!"

In Bud's convertible, the four young people were soon on their way to the Shopton Yacht Club on Lake Carlopa.

The *Mary Nestor* was moored in the club's boat basin. She was a graceful craft with a gleaming hull and sleek lines.

As they hoisted sail and got under way, Tom settled himself in the cockpit and prepared to scan the lake with his field glasses.

It was a perfect day for sailing, with a hot sun sparkling down on the water, and a brisk, spanking breeze. The lake was dotted with sailboats, skimming across the blue, like graceful white sea birds.

As Bud handled the tiller, Tom, with his glasses, studied the occupants of every craft that came into view.

Suddenly he lowered the field glasses and turned to Bud.

"See if you can overhaul that boat I'm pointing to. She keeps pulling away from us every time we get within viewing distance, and the man at the tiller avoids looking in our direction."

Without seeming to have any particular objective in mind, Bud attempted to overtake the boat Tom had indicated. But whenever the *Mary Nestor* showed signs of closing in, the other boat would quickly sail out of range.

"That must be Landis, all right," agreed Bud.

"Whoever he is, he certainly doesn't seem anxious for a meeting," commented Phyl.

The two boats now were engaged in an open chase. Like the *Mary Nestor*, the other boat was a fast sailer. The man at the helm was evidently heading for a public dock, some distance from the yacht club.

The *Mary Nestor*, however, had the wind on the beam. Under Bud's skillful handling, she came within close range of the other boat. The man at the helm was Jerry Landis! As the boats drew alongside, Tom sprang over the gunwales into Landis' craft.

Landis put up a brief resistance. But he obviously had no desire to fight with Tom, because sullenly he allowed his adversary to sail the boat back to the yacht basin as Bud and the girls followed.

A few minutes later Tom faced Landis on shore. "All right, let's have it!" he demanded grimly. "Who paid you to fake that accidental landing yesterday at Swift Enterprises?"

"I don't know what you're talking about!" snarled Landis.

"Look!" said Tom, grabbing him by the front of his jersey. "I wouldn't want to hit you but don't crowd your luck!"

Tom had no intention of harming Landis, but the threat alone had an instant effect. The pilot seemed to break down completely. Covering his face with his hands, he poured out the whole story.

"It wasn't my fault! It was Bronich—Ivor Bronich—he made me do it!"

"What do you mean, he made you do it?" Tom asked coldly.

"I owed him money—lots of money! He could have ruined me! But he said he'd cancel the debt if I would fly him into your experimental station. I

*Tom sprang over the gunwales into Landis' craft*

knew it was against regulations, but—well, I didn't see any serious harm in it."

"Of course not," growled Bud sarcastically. "All he wanted to do was steal the plans of Tom's new invention!"

"I didn't know what he was up to!" whined Landis. "I swear I didn't! He told me he just wanted to test a new anti-radar device he'd invented. And I figured he couldn't do any harm with all the guards and gadgets you've got around that place. It wasn't till I flew him out this morning that I realized that he had stolen the blueprints he was carrying."

"Then what happened?"

"He told me to keep my mouth shut and stop worrying, because he was leaving the country to try an experiment. And when I asked him where, he just laughed and said maybe as far as the South Pole!"

"The South Pole!" Bud exclaimed.

Tom gave his friend a warning look and Bud changed the subject.

"How soon was Bronich going to start?" he asked Landis.

"He didn't tell me."

It was a grim-faced Tom who reported the matter to Harlan Ames later that afternoon at Swift Enterprises.

"What did you do with Landis?" inquired the security chief.

"Took him to police headquarters, but said we wouldn't press charges. However, they're going to hold him for further questioning."

In the days that followed, Ames worked diligently to locate Bronich, but the foreign agent seemed to have disappeared. Tom, in the meantime, redrew his blueprints and speeded up work on his two new blasters to a feverish rate. One morning in their private office, the young inventor and his father were discussing the progress being made on the models.

"Here's a sketch of the launching platform I've designed for the South Pole blaster," Tom said, spreading out a blueprint on his father's desk.

The structure was composed of girders and I beams, and looked somewhat like an upside-down rocket-launching platform. Rails were provided to guide the machine on its take-off.

Mr. Swift studied the drawing carefully.

"I believe this will do the trick, all right, son," he commented. "Of course your machine will only have room for a bare minimum of sheathing around the atomic pile, and that will make things much more difficult. It means the launching will have to be done by remote control to make sure you and the others are exposed as little as possible to dangerous radiation."

Tom nodded thoughtfully. "I've already provided for that, Dad." He went on to describe the remote-control system by which he planned to operate the machine.

"By the way, Tom," added Mr. Swift, "I have something here to show you—something which may come as quite a surprise!"

# CHAPTER 10

# A CRUCIAL TEST

AS TOM LOOKED ON, puzzled, his father beamed open the top desk drawer and drew out a piece of paper which was covered with strange mathematical symbols.

Tom pounced on it with a cry of excitement.

"Dad! Another message from our space friends?"

"Right, son. It was picked up by one of our oscilloscopes at the rocket lab on Fearing Island."

The first such message had been sent by a black, meteorlike missile from outer space, which had landed with pinpoint precision on the grounds of the Swift Enterprises experimental station.

Later messages had been received while Tom was conducting the first successful rocket flights. Some of these messages had saved Tom and Bud from deadly peril while they were rocketing on an orbital course around the earth.

"Have you translated this new one yet, Dad?" asked Tom.

"Not completely. I thought we might work on it together, if you can spare the time. I have a hunch it's an answer to that request we transmitted for information about their bodily structure."

The beings who sent the messages—possibly Martians—had mastered interplanetary travel but needed help in solving the problem of how to penetrate the earth's dense atmosphere.

As Tom pulled up a chair alongside his father's desk, the older man produced two small booklets. One of them he handed to Tom.

These booklets were copies of a space dictionary, in which Mr. Swift had compiled the meaning of all the symbols they had so far been able to translate. It greatly speeded up the job of decoding new messages.

For nearly an hour, father and son pored over the latest communication. Working industriously, each one covered numerous sheets of paper with mathematical calculations in his attempt to translate the message.

Finally they paused and looked at each other with puzzled expressions.

"Any luck, son?" asked Mr. Swift.

"I'm not sure. It—well, it doesn't seem right. How about you?"

"The nearest I can make out is that their bodies are covered with armorlike segments, and they move by crawling along the ground."

Tom groaned and looked at his own results. "Now I *know* something's wrong!"

"Why? How do you make it out?"

"According to my version, they communicate with each other by mental telepathy, and each one has two heads!"

Once again, father and son stared at each other in silent bafflement. Then both roared with laughter!

"Well, you're right about one thing, son," said Mr. Swift when his laughter had subsided to a chuckle. "There certainly must be something wrong with our translations!"

"What I don't understand is how the dickens we came out so differently?"

"I'm afraid it's these new symbols—the ones we haven't received before. They must drastically alter the meaning of the other symbols. But *how?* That's a problem that will take plenty of brainwork."

"Guess it'll have to wait till this South Pole expedition is over," said Tom. With a rueful smile, he crumpled up the papers he had been writing on and tossed them into the wastebasket.

A week later the three government scientists who had been assigned to accompany the expedition arrived at Swift Enterprises. They had been invited to observe the atomic earth blaster on its first real test—the digging of the Pine Hill tunnel.

In the absence of Mr. Swift, who was away on business at the Citadel, the Swifts' atomic energy plant, Tom and Bud acted as a greeting committee for the three visitors.

The oldest member of the trio was Dr. Anton Faber, a world-famous zoologist. He was a tall, slender, gray-haired man, with keen, steel-gray eyes peering out through thick-lensed glasses.

"Allow me to introduce my two companions," he said, after shaking hands with Tom and Bud. "On my right is Daryl Blake, a brilliant young botanist who was most eager to volunteer for this trip."

Blake, a husky, red-haired chap with a grinning, freckled face, promptly stuck out his hand and gave each of the boys a warm handclasp.

"Thanks for the orchids, Doc. But it really is true about my being all het up over this assignment. I'm anxious to experiment with some of those Antarctic plants I've read about."

"I didn't even know they had plants at the South Pole," said Bud.

"Yes, indeed," replied Blake, "and mighty interesting ones, too. Some of them are no bigger than a pinhead because they have only a few hours of sunlight every year in which to grow."

Dr. Faber interrupted with a smile. "Tut-tut, my

dear chap. If you get started on your favorite subject, we may all be standing here till midnight. And
I have yet to introduce the third member of our
party—Mr. Harold Voorhees."

Voorhees was an electrical engineer who special-
ized in thermal measurements. A big, handsome,
powerfully built fellow, with blond hair and light-
blue eyes, he had a smug, self-satisfied air which
caused Bud to take an instant dislike to him.

"Rather young to be engaged in this type of work,
aren't you?" he said, smiling at the boys in a patron-
izing manner.

Bud leaned forward mischievously, pulling one
ear forward, and drawled, "Tell you what, Hal, old
man. Maybe you'd like to take a look and see if
we're dry behind the ears yet."

Voorhees' smile faded abruptly. "I'm afraid that
remains to be seen. Incidentally, I would prefer not
to be called Hal. It's a nickname I've never cared
for."

To smooth over the awkward moment, Tom suggested that they have lunch immediately, then visit
the Swift Construction Company plant for a look at
the nearly completed blasters.

"This one," he announced later that afternoon,
as they examined the huge machines, "is the model
I plan to use for digging the tunnel. Unlike the
other one which you just saw, this will operate me-

chanically rather than by smelting and vaporizing the rock."

Voorhees was scrutinizing the section in which the small atomic pile would later be installed.

"I can tell you right now that you're way off the beam on this part," he scoffed. "The thickness of these heat-transfer walls is entirely inadequate. Of course the correct design depends on certain thermodynamic formulas with which you probably aren't familiar."

"Are these the ones you mean?" asked Tom quietly, pulling out a notebook and rapidly jotting down a number of formulas.

With a startled look, Voorhees glanced at them and admitted grudgingly that they were indeed the ones he had been referring to.

"Perhaps we'd better check them right now," suggested Tom. "If I *have* made a mistake, I certainly want to clear it up as soon as possible."

Using pocket slide rules and a handbook of tables borrowed from one of the company engineers, Tom and Voorhees proceeded to work out the formulas.

Tom was the first to finish. A few minutes later Voorhees also completed his calculations. As he compared his answer with Tom's, his face flushed a dull red.

"Well—hmm—I—uh—seem to have spoken too soon. Your figures seem to be quite correct, after all."

Bud clapped Voorhees on the back and laughed. "Sorry, Hal old boy, but even the greatest minds sometimes have an off day!"

As Dr. Faber coughed loudly, and Daryl Blake turned away to hide a smile, Voorhees glared at Bud furiously.

Three days later, the "cheap steel" blaster was ready to operate. The hour had arrived for the crucial test at Pine Hill.

The news that Tom Swift's new invention would begin tunneling at nine o'clock that morning had been blazoned across the front page of the *Shopton Evening Bulletin* the night before. It had also been announced on all radio and television newscasts.

As a result, the area around Pine Hill was so crowded with people that the police had to be called to hold back the spectators.

All three of the government scientists—Dr. Faber, Blake, and Voorhees—were on hand to watch the proceedings. Tom showed them a blueprint of the proposed tunnel layout.

"The blaster will start from here," he explained, "operating at a downward slope of twenty degrees. Then the machine will level off and continue on a straight course to the center of the hill. After which, we repeat the same operations on the other side of the hill, with the two tunnels joining in the middle."

"How about those long sections of metal tubing?"

asked Blake, pointing to several rows of big tubes neatly stacked for use. "What are they for?"

"As the blaster digs into the hill, those sections of tubing will be connected, one by one, to form a single, long, flexible tube," replied the young inventor. "And the ground-up dirt and rock will be blown out through it."

A picked crew of workmen from Swift Enterprises was standing by, waiting for operations to begin. The blaster itself was poised against the hillside with several sections of tubing already hooked on.

About twenty yards from the blaster, on level ground, was Tom's remote-control shack, mounted on a movable dolly.

As Tom walked to the shack and climbed inside, his heart was hammering with excitement. He knew that everything depended on the outcome of today's test.

Through the window of the control shack, Tom looked at the foreman of the work crew and received an "All Clear" signal in reply.

Taking a deep breath, Tom turned on the starter switch, then pushed down a lever. Instantly the blaster roared into life with a thunderous whine. As the nose end of the machine bit deep into the hillside, a stream of pulverized dirt and rock began to spurt out the rear end of the tube.

Realizing that the long-needed tunnel was at last under way, the crowd broke into a wave of spontaneous cheers and applause. But the noise could scarcely be heard above the din of the blaster.

In a matter of seconds, the machine had burrowed half its length into the hillside on a downward slant.

Suddenly an explosion shook the hillside. The earth blaster and tons of dirt were blown back toward Tom's control shack!

# CHAPTER 11

## SABOTAGE!

SCREAMS AND CRIES arose from the spectators as rocks and dirt pelted down on them. Tom's shack was deluged by the debris. The crippled blaster stopped inches from it!

Tom, white-faced and shaken, leaped outside. Angry shouts greeted him on all sides.

"That crazy machine might have killed every one of us!" bellowed a fat, middle-aged man.

And a woman screamed, "It's a public danger! The police should arrest him!"

Gritting his teeth, Tom tried to ignore the angry remarks. While Bud summoned an ambulance, he proceeded to give first aid to all who needed it, with the help of Dr. Faber and Daryl Blake. Fortunately, the injuries amounted to no more than slight cuts and bruises.

After the victims had been taken care of, Tom turned to the sergeant in charge of the police detail.

"Would you please have your men clear this area? I'd like to make a complete investigation of what happened."

"That's pretty obvious, isn't it?" put in Voorhees. "Your blaster was improperly designed, just as I suspected all along. When it hit bedrock, it couldn't penetrate any farther. So the result was a power blowback."

The police sergeant seemed impressed with this line of reasoning. But Tom shook his head. "I'm quite sure that the accident was not the fault of the blaster."

"Meaning what?" Voorhees asked.

"Meaning someone set a contact bomb to ruin our work here, and perhaps blow me up at the same time!"

"Sounds like that guy Picken to me," commented Bud.

"Could be," Tom said. "We'll have him investigated just to play safe. But I think this job was planned by Bronich. By making the blaster look worthless, he may hope to have the government call off our South Pole expedition."

Anton Faber nodded thoughtfully. The gray-haired scientist and his two associates had already been told about Bronich's activities.

"This certainly bears all the earmarks of sabotage," he agreed. "Your blaster is badly crushed."

A few minutes later Harlan Ames roared up to the scene in a car with four plant guards. After listening to a hasty account of the accident, he ordered his men to fan out over the area and search for clues. Then he and Tom forced their way into the mouth of the tunnel.

With the light of a powerful electric lantern, they examined the forward wall where the blaster had stopped digging. There were unmistakable signs of an explosion.

As the young inventor and his security chief emerged from the tunnel mouth, one of the plant guards came up to show them several bomb fragments.

"Found 'em scattered among the debris," he explained.

That afternoon, when the *Shopton Evening Bulletin* hit the streets with an extra, it carried a full account of the bomb fragments. By releasing the details, Tom hoped to relieve people's minds.

But his troubles were not yet over. Far from soothing public worry, the bomb story seemed to awaken even greater fears.

All through the rest of the afternoon, Swift Enterprises, the Swift Construction Company, and the newspaper itself were swamped with phone calls and telegrams from indignant citizens.

The burden of their complaints was always the same: *Don't let Tom Swift carry out any more of his crazy experiments on public property!*

When the young inventor arrived home that night, he felt drained of energy. Hardly had he sunk down in an easy chair when the telephone jangled.

"You leave this one to me," his sister Sandy called from the telephone alcove. "If it's someone being nasty, I'll bite his head off!"

A moment later she approached her brother with a surprised and slightly uneasy look on her face.

"Tom, it's the mayor! He wants to speak to you."

Tom walked to the telephone and took the receiver. "Yes, sir?"

"Tom, I'm afraid this situation is getting out of hand!" Mayor Drummond sounded worried and harassed. "The public outcry is so bad that half the Town Council wants to call off the whole project."

Tom protested. "But the machine wasn't at fault. The bomb fragments prove that. It was obviously a case of sabotage!"

"That's just the trouble! Some people think that more bombs may have been planted!"

Tom stiffened with a sudden shock of alarm. This was a possibility that had not occurred to him.

"Tell everyone we'll take immediate precautions," he promised. "And I'll report back at once if there's any further sign of danger!"

Calling Harlan Ames, he ordered plant security

men to guard the digging area at all times. Then he contacted Hank Sterling and told him to organize a crew of technicians, armed with mine detectors.

"Drive them out to Pine Hill on a company truck. I'll be waiting for you there."

When Hank and his men arrived, Tom issued crisp orders. "I want every inch of the hillside within a hundred-yard radius of the digging area combed with those detectors!"

"We'll do it pronto," Hank agreed.

The men were assigned to various spots at the proposed entrance and on the mountainside. They began work at once. The onlookers watched anxiously as the searchers moved about the area.

In less than an hour, Hank reported the area free of danger.

"Fine!" said Tom. "Now let's try the other side of the hill." The site of the opposite entrance to the proposed tunnel has been clearly marked by the surveyors. Tom waited tensely as the crew fanned out with their electronic detectors.

Suddenly one of the men called. Tom and Hank ran to his side. Transferring the earphones to his own head, Tom heard a loud buzzing noise. It meant metal was nearby. A bomb? he wondered.

"All right, clear everyone away from here," ordered the young inventor.

Hank gripped his shoulder. "Listen, Tom, these

contact bombs are mighty tricky. Some go off on a hair trigger. Why not call the FBI and leave this job to a professional bomb-disposal squad?"

Tom shook his head stubbornly. "That bomb spells danger every second it stays there. Besides, calling in someone else would just be passing the buck. This is my project, so it's up to me to take the risks!"

Tom bent over the suspected spot, and working with a featherlight touch, began brushing away the dirt. Finally a piece of black metal came into view.

"It's a bomb, all right!" he muttered grimly.

Tom's forehead was beaded with perspiration. Holding his breath, he proceeded to disarm the fuse. Hank Sterling and his men were watching tensely from a safe distance. An audible sigh of relief rose from the group when they saw that Tom now had deactivated the bomb. This was followed by a ringing cheer.

As Hank rushed forward to congratulate him, Tom sagged limply.

"Nice work, Tom!" cried the blond, square-jawed engineer, throwing an arm around the young inventor's shoulders.

When he arrived home Tom called Mayor Drummond. He expected that the official would be greatly relieved to hear that the digging area was now completely safe. But again he was in for an unpleasant surprise.

"I'm sorry to tell you this, Tom," said Mayor Drummond, "but certain members of the council have forced a showdown. We're taking a vote tomorrow morning on whether or not to halt your project!"

**CHAPTER 12**

# A FLIGHT TO ALASKA

TENSELY AWAITING the outcome of the council's vote, a group of friends gathered in Tom's office the next morning.

"If those chowderheads decide to stop you from digging," Bud growled, "the public ought to make them scratch out that tunnel themselves—with spoons and nail files!"

Tom, in spite of his anxiety, gave a wry smile but said nothing.

By eleven o'clock there was still no word from Town Hall. Another fifteen minutes went by, then another.

"Brand my thermopile! What's keepin' them sidewinders?" exclaimed Chow nervously.

"Must be a close fight," Hank Sterling remarked, "which makes me hopeful."

A few minutes before twelve, the phone rang. Everyone jumped but Tom. The young inventor's face was grim and expressionless as he took the call.

"Hello? . . . Oh, yes, Mayor Drummond. . . . They did, eh? Well, thanks very much for your support. . . . Sure thing. . . . Good-by, sir."

There was dead silence as Tom hung up the phone. For a moment he rubbed his hand over his eyes, and his shoulders seemed to droop.

Finally Bud spoke. "Thumbs down?"

To everybody's surprise, Tom looked up with a grin of relief.

"Thumbs *up*, pal! They just voted to let us continue digging!"

With the sudden release of tension, everyone began laughing and talking at once, as they gathered around to clap Tom on the back and offer congratulations. But Tom knew the real test was just beginning.

Within twenty-four hours, the bomb damage to the blaster had been repaired, and the digging was resumed. This time, there were few spectators on hand. And the ones who did appear were tight-lipped and unfriendly.

Results of the first day's work, nevertheless, were highly encouraging, and by the end of a full week of operations, the mid-point of the tunnel had been reached.

Now the tide of public opinion in Shopton began to turn in Tom's favor. As work continued on the opposite half of the tube, more and more onlookers were showing up every morning.

On the day scheduled for the final break-through, a civic ceremony was staged at Pine Hill. On hand were the mayor and the rest of the Town Council.

With Tom at the controls, the blaster plowed through the last few yards of earth separating the two halves of the tunnel.

The moment the nose of the machine broke through the last remaining barrier, a red light flashed outside the control shack and an alarm bell started ringing. Elated, Tom smiled as the crowd went wild, shouting and clapping their approval.

Mayor Drummond capped the climax with a brief speech praising the young scientist and his achievements. Again the crowd burst into wild applause.

Chow Winkler, however, looked on sourly. He had not forgotten that only a short time ago many of these same people had been calling his beloved young boss a public menace.

Now that the first cut was completed, and a shaft had been driven all the way through the hill, work progressed rapidly in widening the tunnel to full size. Then a construction gang moved in to line the tunnel with steel and concrete.

About a week after the ceremony at Pine Hill,

Tom held a meeting in his private office with Blake, Faber, and Voorhees, to talk over final plans for the South Pole expedition. Bud was also present.

"You realize, I hope," said Voorhees in a condescending voice, "that we *senior* scientists must take along a good deal of equipment. And as representatives of the Federal government, *our* things will have top priority over all other cargo. Now then, how will this equipment be transported?"

Tom exchanged an amused glance with Bud before answering.

"I'm sure there'll be ample cargo space on our planes, Mr. Voorhees. But I'm glad you brought up the matter. I suggest that you give me a complete list of your equipment as soon as possible, so we can start making our stowage plans."

"Blake and I have our equipment all boxed and ready," Dr. Faber announced quietly. "Here is a list of everything we're taking. I trust there will still be room for your atomic earth blaster."

His gray eyes twinkled behind their thick-lensed spectacles. Tom grinned as he realized that this distinguished scientist considered Voorhees something of a stuffed shirt—just as he and Bud did!

"By the way, Doctor," said the young inventor, "perhaps you and your friends would like to see the layout of our Flying Lab—the *Sky Queen*."

"Delighted!" Faber murmured.

Leading his guests to the underground hangar, Tom beamed open the sliding steel door with his electronic key. They followed him down a flight of steps. On the hangar floor below stood a great silver airplane with rakish, swept-back wings.

The *Sky Queen* had already carried Tom and his friends on a number of amazing adventures.

Atomic-powered, the huge ship was a flying laboratory, equipped with all the latest scientific instruments. Normally it carried a small jet plane called the *Kangaroo Kub*, as well as the *Skeeter*, a jet-lifted helicopter.

The laboratory area was located amidships on the second deck of the plane. Both soundproof and air-conditioned, it was divided into a number of cubicles. Each compartment was equipped for some special field of scientific study.

"How do you like it?" Tom asked Daryl Blake, as he showed him the botany compartment.

The red-haired, freckle-faced scientist stared in amazement at the microscopes, the plant-growing tanks, the well-stocked shelves of chemical nutrients for hydroponic experiments, and all the other numerous items of equipment.

"Why, it's out of this world!" he exclaimed. "With a setup like this, I'll be able to do anything in the Antarctic that I can do in my own lab in Washington!"

Dr. Faber was equally thrilled by the zoology lab. "This plane is a scientist's dream come true!" he declared.

"Since it has these compartments set up for your types of work, I believe you two may as well fly with me on the *Sky Queen*," Tom told them. He also decided that Voorhees would ride with Bud Barclay on one of the jet cargo planes.

Bud groaned when Tom informed him of this decision later that afternoon.

"Oh, for Pete's sake! You mean I'm stuck with that pompous windbag all the way from here to the South Pole?"

"Relax, chum!" The young inventor smiled. "At jet speed, the flight won't take long. By the way, your plane will be equipped with two sets of landing wheels."

Bud looked puzzled. "How come?"

"One will be your regular landing gear, and the other will be a special set of wheels armed with metal spikes for landing on ice. The plane will also carry ski runners for landing or taking off on snow."

"Have you figured out how many planes to take on the expedition?"

"Four altogether, I think. Besides the *Sky Queen* and the craft you fly, there will be two more jet cargo planes. I'm putting you in charge of those, as well as your own ship."

Tom went on to explain that the cargo jets would carry the extra clothing and food supplies; machines for carving out an ice dome to house the men; other tools of various kinds; an air conditioner for warming and ventilating the ice cave; tractors and snowmobiles; and last but not least, an extra blaster.

"What's that for?" inquired Bud.

"Safety precaution. There's always a chance the main blaster may be crushed or pinned by a sudden shift in the earth's crust. Or the shaft might be blocked off. Either way, we'd be stymied without a spare machine on hand."

"I see what you mean," said Bud. "Speaking of the main blaster, I suppose you'll carry that in the *Sky Queen?*"

"Right. Also the helicopter. But I think we'll leave the *Kangaroo Kub* behind on this trip."

Bud drummed his fingers thoughtfully on the desk before resuming the conversation.

"You know, skipper, I've been wondering if it might not be smart to take along some huskies and dog sleds on this expedition. They could take us anywhere—places we couldn't go even in a snowmobile. And dogs never stall or freeze up on you, as engines sometimes do."

Tom nodded. "An excellent idea, Bud. Of course, if we did take dog teams along, we'd have to transport them in a sort of flying kennel."

Bud approved of this idea, and begged to be given the job of flying such a plane. After discussing the matter for a while, Tom agreed to this arrangement.

It was also decided to fly to Alaska the following day to purchase huskies and sleds.

"We can take Sandy and Phyl along, and make it a day's outing," Tom suggested.

"Now you're talking like a *real* genius, pal! Let's give the girls a call this very minute!"

At nine o'clock the next morning the *Sky Queen* was rolled from the underground hangar. When it was ready for take-off, Tom, Bud, and the girls climbed aboard the mammoth silver plane.

Tom gunned the nuclear engines into life. A moment later, as he poured power into the jet lifters, the huge ship rose into the air.

Sandy and Phyl sat up front in the pilot's compartment with the boys.

"Where in Alaska do you plan to buy your huskies?" asked Phyl as they streaked across the continent at a speed faster than sound.

"From an Indian named Colonel George Eagle Friend," replied Tom.

"Goodness, that's quite a name!"

"He's quite a man, from what Dad tells me. Colonel Friend has a wonderful war record, and now he makes a business of breeding sled dogs. He and Dad are old friends."

At noontime Tom set the huge plane down on the airfield at Fairbanks, Alaska. It was strange to feel the bite of winter in the air when they stepped from the plane.

The foursome ate lunch at a local restaurant, then took a taxi to the kennels, which were located a short distance from town.

Colonel Eagle Friend, a full-blooded Alaskan Indian, greeted them with delight. He was a splendid figure of a man, tall and straight as an arrow, with a shock of blue-black hair and twinkling black eyes.

"*Klahowya!* Welcome to Alaska! I'm only sorry that Tom Senior didn't come with you!"

When they were comfortably seated inside his rambling log bungalow, Tom told him the reason for their visit.

"We'd like to buy a good dog team and all the necessary equipment. You see, we're planning an expedition to the South Pole."

The colonel's eyebrows rose in surprise. "Another one, eh?"

Tom was puzzled. "What do you mean? This will be the first trip to the South Pole we've ever made."

"What I meant was, I just sold an outfit to another fellow who's going there," the Indian explained. "Maybe you know him."

## CHAPTER 13

## DOG TROUBLE

"WHAT'S HIS NAME?" Tom asked, startled by the news.

"He called himself Smith," the Indian replied, "but I doubt that's his real name because he had a heavy accent."

"Bronich, I'll bet!" Bud groaned, as Tom quickly gave Colonel Eagle Friend a description of the subversive Kranjovian.

"That's the man," the Indian said. "Your description fits him perfectly. I take it you've crossed his trail before!"

"Most of the time, he's been crossing ours!" Bud declared. "That secret invention he was boasting about really belongs to Tom. Bronich stole the plans for it from Swift Enterprises!"

"He's actually a secret agent of the Kranjovian

116

government," Tom added, "wanted by the FBI for espionage and on several other counts. Now it looks as if he's trying to beat us to the South Pole!"

The young inventor told the colonel about his atomic earth blaster and his plans for tapping iron from the center of the earth.

"Well, at least I can outfit you with a good team of huskies," said the Indian. "I'll give you the best dogs in my kennel."

Slipping on their coats again, the boys and girls accompanied their host out to the back of his cabin, where the huskies were kept in wire-enclosed runs.

At Colonel Eagle Friend's approach, the dogs set up a loud, eager barking, jumping up against the wire and wagging their tails frantically. They were of various sizes and mostly black, white, or wolf gray in color. All had slant eyes and a thick ruff of fur around their necks, as well as curling, bushy tails.

"How big a team do you want?" inquired the colonel, turning to the boys.

"What do you advise?" replied Tom.

The Indian thought for a moment. "Well, nine dogs are enough even for the heaviest loads. But I'll give you two more dogs for spares. Then, if you like, you can split them into two smaller teams for light hauling."

Opening a gate, he went into one of the runs and brought out a small, wiry husky with a mask of

silver-white fur around the eyes and muzzle, out-
lined by blackish fur on the head and ears.

"This is Klootch," he announced. "She'll be your
lead dog."

"I thought lead dogs were supposed to be big and
powerful," Bud said.

"It's more important to have one that's smart and
fast. And Klootch is all of that. She's a Siberian
husky."

So that the boys might accustom themselves to
handling a dog team, Colonel Eagle Friend hitched
up two outfits—one for Tom and one for Bud.

As the boys mounted the sled runners and grasped
the handle bars, he called, "All set?"

"Sure." Bud grinned. "But how do you start these
rigs?"

"Like this," replied the Indian. With a crack of
his long rawhide whip, he shouted, "Mush!" Instantly the dogs strained against the harness and the
sleds glided away.

"Hey, this is almost as much fun as riding a jet!"
yelled Bud. "Let's make it a race, chum!"

"You're on, driver!"

Picking up the whips from their sleds, the boys
cracked them in the air and shouted words of en-
couragement to their teams.

The dogs put on speed, stretching their legs farther and faster with every stride. Soon the sleds

seemed to be flying over the snow! Cheeks red from the stinging wintry air, the boys laughed and yelled back and forth.

Neither was aware that the huskies were gradually getting out of hand. The sleds carried no loads, and the dogs sensed the inexperience of their drivers.

Soon they came to a dip in the terrain, where a high, steep hillside sloped down to a frozen creek bed.

"Look out, Bud!" Tom shouted. "Whoa! Whoa, you huskies!"

Tom had suddenly realized that the teams were running away.

Bud, too, tried frantically to stop his team. But the dogs paid no heed. At headlong speed, they went racing down the slope.

A moment later one of Bud's sled runners hit a boulder. The jarring jolt caused the sled to turn over, throwing Bud against a nearby tree trunk!

Rocketing down the hill at breakneck speed, Tom, too, lost his footing on the sled runners. As his legs spun out from under him, his hands slipped from the bars. Over and over he hurtled down the icy hillside!

At the bottom, he lay dazed for a minute or two before struggling painfully to his feet. Halfway up the hillside, Bud was sprawled, motionless, at the foot of a tree. Just as Tom reached his friend and began to chafe his wrists, another dog team came into view. The colonel was riding the sled. He halted his dogs on the brow of the hill, and jumping from the runners, hurried toward the boys. When he saw that Bud's forehead bore a dark bruise, he said:

"I was afraid this might happen when I saw you start racing. That's why I followed."

Bud soon revived and grinned sheepishly at his own plight. "Looks as if huskies are even trickier to handle than a jet!" he muttered.

"Especially on loops and wing overs," remarked the Indian, as the corners of his mouth twitched in a faint smile.

After the dog breeder had recovered the runaway teams, the boys drove them carefully back to the cabin.

*The jolt caused the sled to turn over,*

As Tom and Bud were washing up and treating their scrapes and bruises with antiseptic, Bud remarked, "Doggone, that old Eagle Eye is a real swell Joe. I wish he could come with us on the expedition!"

"Great minds run in the same channel!" Tom grinned. "I was just wishing the same thing. Why don't we ask him?"

Over a tasty snack which Mrs. Eagle Friend prepared for her guests before their departure, Tom

*throwing Bud against a tree trunk*

broached the question. In reply, the Indian said:

"I've been hoping you'd ask me ever since I heard about the expedition. But, of course, before I give you an answer, I'll have to talk this over with my wife."

For several minutes, Colonel and Mrs. Eagle Friend conversed in their native Indian dialect. Finally the colonel turned to Tom with a smile.

"She says all right, provided I keep myself bundled up nice and warm!"

Everyone laughed, and Sandy added, "I think it's wonderful that you're going along on the expedition, Colonel Eagle Friend! Now I feel better about the boys going, too, because I'm sure you'll keep an eye on them!"

After leaving instructions with his wife for the care and feeding of the huskies, the Indian drove his four young companions to the airport. They rode in a rickety old sedan with a huge trailer hitched in back, carrying the eleven dogs and equipment selected for the expedition.

At sight of the *Sky Queen,* the Indian muttered in awe, *"Skookum kallakalla!"*

"Come again?" Bud said, blinking.

"In the Chinook tongue that means *mighty bird,"* explained the colonel. "And never have I seen a plane which more deserved the title!"

Tom showed him the cargo stowage space on the

first deck, then, with Sandy and Phyllis, he went top-side to contact Shopton via short-wave radio.

"What do you plan on doing with the dogs?" Bud asked the colonel. "Just turn 'em loose here in this cargo compartment?"

The Indian shook his head. "They'd be at each other's throats the moment you did so. I think the safest plan will be to partition them off in separate stalls."

With lumber which he had brought along in the trailer, he proceeded to put together some crude wooden stalls, one for each dog. With Bud helping him, the job was quickly completed.

Meanwhile, Tom had made radio contact with his father back at Swift Enterprises. He told him of Bronich's visit to Colonel Eagle Friend, and the spy's boast about mining ore at the South Pole.

"Looks as if we'll have to move fast, Dad, if we don't want Bronich to beat us to the punch. How are things coming at the plant?"

"Good shape, son. Hank Sterling says the main blaster should be ready for testing tomorrow."

"Swell, Dad! That's great news! In the meantime, how about contacting Washington for final clearance?"

Mr. Swift promised to do so immediately, and Tom signed off. A short time later the huge plane headed back to Shopton.

As darkness fell over the continent, the *Sky Queen* streaked across western Canada, through the star-studded night skies.

Colonel Eagle Friend was seated in the pilot's compartment with the young people.

"Hope you won't mind my calling you Eagle Eye," remarked Bud.

"Not at all," chuckled the Indian. "My full name is a bit long."

Just then Phyl said, "Hey! Sounds as if something's going on down in the cargo space!"

Tom snapped an intercom switch. Instantly the loud-speaker blared out a bloodcurdling noise of dogs howling, yapping, and snarling!

The Indian leaped up. "The huskies!" he exclaimed. "At least one of them must have broken loose—maybe more! Dogs sometimes go berserk in planes and kill anything in sight!"

# CHAPTER 14

# A CALL FROM WASHINGTON

THE UPROAR of the angry huskies was deafening! Quickly Colonel Eagle Friend scrambled down the steel-runged ladder leading to the first deck.

Tom snapped off the intercom and set the ship on automatic pilot. Then he and the others hurried to join the Indian outside the cargo compartment.

"Good night!" shuddered Sandy, putting her hands to her ears. "It sounds as if the dogs are killing one another!"

The colonel, who also was a trained veterinarian, was taking something out of his medical kit.

"What are you going to do?" Bud asked.

"Those are fine dogs," Eagle Friend replied. "I don't want to shoot any of them unless I have to. So I'll try this first." He held up a can of chloroform so they could read the label, then loosened the cap.

125

"Now open the door to the cargo space," he ordered.

As Tom did so, the Indian quickly removed the cap and tossed the open can in among the wrangling huskies.

Instantly Tom bolted the door and almost at once the clamor of the dogs began to die down. Soon it ceased completely.

"I'll go in now and attend to them," said the Indian. "But first, I advise you young people to go back to the pilot's compartment. When I open this door, the smell of chloroform will just about knock you over!"

"Don't worry," Tom said, smiling. "The exhaust fans of our air-conditioning system will take care of that. If you think the dogs are unconscious, I'll air the ship out now."

When the Indian nodded, the young inventor turned a knob on the control panel. Instantly the ventilator fans hummed, forcing the bad air from the *Sky Queen*.

"All right, I think it's safe now," the Indian announced. Accompanied by Tom and Bud, he made his way into the cargo compartment. Most of the dogs were still sleeping; some were partly conscious. Three were gashed and bleeding from the fangs of the half-crazed husky that had broken into the other stalls.

The Indian dressed their wounds and made them

comfortable, murmuring reassuring words to them in native dialect as he worked.

"How long will they stay groggy?" Tom asked.

"Another couple of hours at least. In any case, they're all securely tied now, so I think there's nothing more to worry about."

It was past midnight when they arrived back at Shopton. The air seemed warm and muggy after the bracing climate of Alaska.

"I'm afraid the change of climate may be pretty hard on the dogs," said the colonel with a worried look.

"Tell you what," said Tom. "We have plenty of room in our low-temperature lab at Enterprises. It's as big as an airplane hangar. Why not arrange kennels for them in there?"

The Indian approved of this idea. When the plane landed, he transported the wobbly huskies to the low-temperature laboratory. Tom's workmen hastily built kennels for the animals and set up comfortable quarters for the Alaskan to watch them.

The next day, Tom's improved atomic drill was moved from the Swift Construction Company plant to a huge shed on the grounds of Swift Enterprises. Here the pile was installed and the finishing touches put on the borer.

Now, under Hank Sterling's watchful eye, the blaster was raised off the ground by powerful chain hoists and dollies slipped underneath. Then the whole assembly was pulled out of the shed by a big, rubber-tired tractor and hauled to the testing ground.

"So yo're finally gonna test out this here monster bug, eh?" asked Chow, as he watched the preparations.

"That's right," Tom said. "Keep your fingers crossed and let's hope she comes through with flying colors."

"Son, I'll do more'n that. I'll keep *everythin'* crossed, includin' my eyes!"

A crane lifted the blaster off the dollies and eased it into position on the launching platform. Elaborate precautions had been taken to guard against dangerous radiation. The platform was surrounded by Tomasite shields, and a special blower duct had been set up to draw off the hot gases.

Mr. Swift, Blake, Voorhees, and Dr. Faber were on hand for the test, as well as numerous plant employees. They watched in silence as Tom climbed into the remote-control booth.

Trying to remain calm, Tom snapped on the main switch, then started feeding power into the machine.

At first there was a smooth, steady whine as the blaster plowed downward into the earth. But a moment later came a thunderous, ear-shattering roar like a thousand pneumatic hammers ripping into concrete! Under the impact, the control booth and the surrounding ground began to vibrate and shudder!

Quickly Tom shut off the blaster and climbed out of the booth to find out what was wrong.

"Well, what now?" inquired Voorhees smugly. "Another contact bomb?"

Bud gave him a withering look.

Tom consulted with his father.

"I believe we'd better remove the blaster and examine the shaft," the elder inventor suggested.

Tom donned a safety suit and climbed down into the shaft to make the examination. When he returned to the surface and pulled off his plastic headgear, he was smiling.

"Did you find the cause?" Mr. Swift asked.

"There's a shelf of basaltic bedrock down there we never knew about. The rock transmits vibrations in all directions. No wonder we got shaken up when the blaster bit into it!"

The earth blaster was now replaced in position, and boring resumed until the shaft was three or four yards deeper. Although the vibration continued, there was no doubt that the blaster itself was operating perfectly!

Congratulations greeted Tom from all sides as he turned off the motor and stepped from the control booth.

"Bud, I'm ready to start packing for the Antarctic,

right now!" announced the young inventor triumphantly.

Later that afternoon, Miss Trent summoned him to the main building to take a phone call from Senator Rives at Washington. Tom lifted the receiver. "Hello?"

"Tom," the senator said, "I'm afraid I have bad news for you. You'll have to call off your South Pole trip!"

**CHAPTER 15**

# SOUTHWARD HO!

THE SHOCKING NEWS that his polar expedition might be called off stunned Tom. "But, Senator Rives," he said, "the government promised financial support and gave us full clearance for the expedition!"

"I know that, Tom. As senator from your state, I supported your father's proposal and helped win official backing for the idea."

"Then why the sudden reversal?"

"No use trying to explain over the phone. I suggest that you come to Washington. Then I can show you just what we're up against."

Mr. Swift shared his son's keen disappointment and wished him success on his trip to the capital. Early the next morning Tom boarded a company jet, and a short time later set the ship down at the

Washington airport. From there, he taxied to the Senate Office Building. A secretary ushered him into Senator Rives' private office.

The senator, a portly, gray-haired man, rose to shake hands and invited the young inventor to sit down.

"Before you say anything," he began, "take a look at this stack of letters and telegrams." With a tap of his hand, the senator indicated a mass of correspondence piled on one corner of his desk.

Tom glanced through a few of them. *Every one was an urgently worded demand that the government call off any plans for deep-digging operations at the South Pole!*

"No use reading the rest of them," said Senator Rives. "They're all the same. The people who sent those complaints are afraid your plans to tap the earth's core may cause volcanoes—tidal waves— even the end of the world!"

"That's ridiculous!" Tom protested.

"The government doesn't think so."

"What do you mean?"

"The same authorities who first granted permission," Senator Rives went on, "now want the expedition delayed. They say they want time to study the matter further."

Tom groaned in despair. "Isn't there anything we can do—any way we can change their minds?"

The senator shook his head gloomily. "I'm afraid not. The authorities are fearful of angering the public."

Tom frowned, giving the problem intense thought. Finally he said, "Senator, have you ever heard of Dr. Roy MacGregor?"

"Scientist of some kind, isn't he?"

"Yes," Tom said. "Probably the foremost meteorologist in the country. He also happens to be a close friend of my father's. Suppose he were to come along with us on the expedition. He could keep in constant touch with seismological stations all over the world. And if anyone reported the slightest sign of trouble due to our operations, we'd stop drilling at once."

The senator got up from his desk and paced around the room. "Well, Tom, it's a good idea," he said. "I'll talk it over with the authorities and see if they'll change their minds."

"Thanks, Senator Rives!" Tom exclaimed, as they shook hands. After he left the Senate Office Building, he went directly to the Federal Bureau of Investigation, where both he and his father were known. He asked to see an agent with whom he had had many previous contacts.

"What brings you to Washington, Tom?" inquired the FBI man when the young inventor was seated in his office.

Tom described his plans to drill for iron at the South Pole, and told how the expedition was now being balked by a flood of public protests. He also mentioned the activities of Ivor Bronich.

"I have a hunch," Tom went on, "that a lot of those complaints may have been inspired either by Bronich himself or other Kranjovian agents. By getting the United States government to call off *our* expedition, they hope to have a free hand in grabbing that ore for themselves."

The FBI man nodded. "Wouldn't be the first time they've pulled that kind of stunt. Subversive organizations often try to influence Congressmen and other government officials by high-pressure mail campaigns."

"If I gave you a list of the people who sent those letters and telegrams," said Tom, "would you have your local agents check them for me?"

"Glad to. But it'll take several days."

Tom thanked him, then stopped at a nearby hotel, where he called Senator Rives' office and asked the secretary to send the FBI the list of names. Next, he made a long-distance call to Grandyke University, where Dr. Roy MacGregor did research in meteorology. Tom told the scientist about his South Pole plans and asked him to join the expedition. Dr. MacGregor accepted the offer with enthusiasm.

"By the way," the meteorologist added, "there's a

government seismologist right there in Washington who recently returned from the Antarctic. His name is Dorset. I understand he made a cruise down there on a Navy cutter, checking up on volcanic disturbances and earthquake tremors. Why not have a talk with him? He's now employed by the National Bureau of Standards."

"Fine!" Tom said. "I'll go see him at once."

He took a taxi and was soon in conference with the man. Dorset was interested to hear of Tom's plans and proved helpful. He even suggested a good spot for a base camp.

"In my opinion, your best bet is somewhere along the foot of these mountains," the seismologist said, pointing to an area on the map west of the great Ross ice barrier. "I flew over this territory in a Navy plane while studying the Mount Erebus volcano."

"Thanks. I'll look it over," Tom said, adding, "An ice-free lake has been reported somewhere among those mountains, hasn't it?"

"Right," Dorset replied. "That may be a sign your molten iron is particularly close to the surface in that vicinity. I'd say it should be a good area to investigate."

Tom thanked Mr. Dorset for the valuable information that he had given him, then hurried to the airport, where he took off in his jet. But as Tom streaked toward Shopton, he chafed at the delay in his plans. Every day lost meant an added advantage for Bronich and the Kranjovians! By the time he reached home, Tom had come to a decision. At a meeting with his father and Uncle Ned in the Enterprises office, Tom said:

"I'd like to go on ahead in the *Sky Queen* to survey a site for our main camp."

"What about the rest of the expedition?" Mr. Swift asked.

"It can follow later, Dad," Tom said, "if and when Senator Rives gets new permission from the government."

As the two older men exchanged glances, the young inventor's jaw set determinedly. "Dad, this is a gamble we've got to take! If we don't, we stand to lose to Bronich!"

"Okay, son, you have my permission," Mr. Swift said, smiling.

"Second the motion," Uncle Ned added. "And good luck to you."

The following day, all hands worked furiously in making final preparations for the take-off. The *Sky Queen* was checked and double-checked from nose to tail. The main blaster and other equipment were also carefully inspected. Then the job of loading the great ship began.

Tom decided that one of the new atomic jet cargo planes should accompany him, piloted by Arvid

Hanson, Enterprises' expert modelmaker who was also a trained flier.

On board the *Sky Queen*, Tom would carry Blake, Faber, Voorhees, Chow, and a crew of five technicians. Two other crewmen would fly with Arvid Hanson.

That evening a farewell party was held at the Swift home, attended by Bud and the Newtons. There were gay decorations and rousing songs. But there was an underlying note of sadness.

"Do you think you can be home by Christmas, son?" Mrs. Swift asked, trying hard to keep her voice cheerful.

"I'm afraid not, Mother," Tom replied. "But you can be sure of one thing—I'll come back just as fast as I can!"

Tom had arranged to have Sandy buy Christmas presents both for relatives and friends—particularly Phyllis Newton. And he had commissioned Bud to buy a present for Sandy before leaving for the South Pole.

Early the next morning the *Sky Queen* was elevated from the underground hangar and readied for flight. Tom's family, accompanied by Phyl and Bud, stood by to watch the take-off.

"Sure wish I was going with you!" said Bud wistfully, as they shook hands.

"Don't worry, flyboy, you'll soon be joining us.

And on your way down, take good care of the pooches!"

Tom waved a last good-by from the pilot's compartment of the *Sky Queen* as the nuclear engines roared into life. With a blast of power from the jet lifters, the great silver ship soared up into the blue.

Traveling through the skies at fourteen hundred miles an hour, Tom watched cities, jungles, and mountains unfold below, then broad stretches of ocean. Ten hours later he caught his first glimpse of the vast and perilous south polar land!

The sky was gray and foggy, and the sea looked the color of lead. But the awe-inspiring spectacle of rugged, towering mountain peaks more than made up for the gloomy atmosphere.

The shores were edged with pack ice. As Tom and his companions watched through powerful binoculars, they made out numerous flocks of penguins, as well as several spouting whales.

Soon they were crossing the Ross Sea, one of the two great gateways to the interior of the Antarctic. Southward, toward the Pole, the sea was bounded by the huge and glittering Ross Barrier.

At the western end of the Barrier, they sighted a volcanic peak emitting plumes of smoke. Tom recognized this as Mount Erebus, and from there on checked his charts frequently for the position recommended by Dorset as a good base.

As the *Sky Queen* drew close to the location, Daryl Blake cried out, "Look! Huskies!"

Using his own binoculars, Tom scanned the whiteness below and quickly spotted a string of sled dogs! Banking sharply, he swooped down for closer scrutiny.

Suddenly his view was blanked out by a pelting blizzard. The plane shuddered violently as winds of tornado velocity spun it around!

## CHAPTER 16

# LOST IN THE BLIZZARD

THE JOLTING SHOCK knocked some of the crew down. Others were slammed against the plane's bulkheads.

With nerveless skill, Tom fought the controls and righted the ship in a slow roll. But the giant plane continued to yaw and pitch violently in the blasting winds.

"For the love of Mike, what happened?" Voorhees gasped as he struggled to regain his balance.

"Polar blizzard," Tom replied tersely. "We ran smack into the teeth of it—or it ran into us!"

Watching the instrument dials carefully, Tom poured atomic power into the jet lifters. Instantly the great ship roared skyward, up through the inky gloom of the storm clouds, then leveled off high above the overcast.

Hanson's jet, which had dogged their trail all the way from the States, was nowhere in sight.

Tom flipped the intercom switch and spoke to the radioman.

"Still in touch with Hanson?"

"Yes, sir. We lost contact for a while when the blow first hit, but now their signal's coming through fine."

"Good! Stay tuned to their frequency and try to maintain contact till we get through this blizzard."

"Roger!"

For the next few hours, Tom flew back and forth over a radius of several hundred miles, seeking a break in the overcast through which to come down. But the storm seemed to be blanketing the entire polar area.

Time hung heavy, and the restlessness and impatience of the *Sky Queen*'s passengers increased hour by hour. The sun moved in the sky, but remained in sight at all times, providing the travelers with a continuous glow of weak, watery light, even though it was now past midnight!

"Blast my infrared cookstove!" grumbled the usually good-natured Chow. "We coulda come by way o' Texas an' stopped off to see the big Panhandle Rodeo in all the time we're wastin' hunkerin' 'round up here!"

It was shortly after two in the morning when the

radioman notified Tom that he had lost contact with Hanson's plane.

"How long since you last heard their signal?" inquired the young inventor.

"About fifteen minutes ago. They seemed to conk out all of a sudden."

"Okay, keep trying and let me know the minute you pick up anything."

Again Tom began combing the polar sky. This time, he flew a definite search pattern, hoping to catch a glimpse of Hanson's cargo jet. But there was no sign of the missing plane.

Finally the storm abated, and the overcast showed signs of clearing. Easing off on the jet lifters, Tom maneuvered the ship cautiously downward through the billowing cloud masses. As the rugged snowscape of the Antarctic continent gradually came into view below them, the great craft slowly settled, until it came to rest on the ice with a gentle bump.

Tom breathed a sigh of relief. His crew also was glad the trip was over. Exhausted from lack of sleep, most of them tumbled into their bunks to snatch a few hours of much-needed rest.

Since there had been no darkness, there was no daybreak to signal the coming of morning. Time had to be judged solely by the clock. At eight Tom put in a radio call to Shopton. Soon his father's voice came back by short wave.

"Great to hear from you, son! Did you have a successful flight?"

Tom described the blizzard they had been through, and told how they had lost contact with Arvid Hanson.

"I've been wondering if you might have picked up his signal back at Shopton?"

"Not so far," replied Mr. Swift. "But I'll keep a radio operator on the job at all times, in case he does try to get through."

"How about Senator Rives?" Tom asked. "Any news yet from Washington?"

"No, nothing from that quarter, either," his father replied. "And I might add that I've still had no luck translating that message from our space friends. The more I work at it, the more puzzling it grows!"

After transmitting several messages for various other members of the crew, Tom signed off and turned the set over to his regular radioman. Just as he was about to descend to the galley for breakfast, the radio operator gave an excited cry.

"Hey, skipper!"

Tom wheeled around instantly and was back at the operator's side in two quick strides.

"Hanson?"

"Yeah, it's Arv, all right! But the signal's weak."

Slipping on the extra earphones, Tom listened anxiously while the operator tried to coax stronger reception from the set. Gradually Hanson's voice came through more clearly.

"Arv!" shouted Tom. "You're safe! But what the dickens happened?"

"Slight accident," replied the modelmaker. "We located a break in the storm around two o'clock this morning and tried to come down. But the overcast made landing in the snow pretty tricky—there were no shadows to outline the shape of things below."

"Did you crack up?"

"Not exactly. But we bellied right across the top of a snow-covered mountain and got hung up. That damaged the undercarriage, and when we finally did get loose, the plane slid down the slope out of control."

"Where are you now?"

"At the foot of the mountain, near open water."

"The Ross Sea?"

"Right. I think I've fixed our position pretty close."

Hanson proceeded to give Tom his approximate latitude and longitude on the chart.

"All right. We'll try to make it there as soon as possible and give you a hand!"

Dashing back to the pilot's compartment, Tom gunned the atomic engines for a take-off. Then, feeding a steady surge of power to the jet lifters, he guided the ship skyward and streaked off across the Antarctic wastes on the rescue mission!

## CHAPTER 17

# BLIND RESCUE

AS TOM'S *Sky Queen* raced to the rescue of the crippled cargo plane, a dense fog began drifting down from the north.

"It's getting thicker every minute," commented Dr. Faber, who was seated beside Tom.

"I'd better switch on the radar," Tom said. "This is a real pea-souper."

Daryl Blake stepped into the compartment. "Think you can find Hanson?" he asked.

"I hope so," Tom replied. "We have his position. But we'll have to get there on instruments if this fog continues."

Tom divided his attention between the altimeter and the radarscope. The plane was skirting a jagged range of mountains, and he knew that an error in judgment could spell quick disaster. Suddenly he hauled up the nose of the plane and jerked open the throttle.

The upward *swoosh* took Faber and Blake by surprise. As they clawed for balance, they saw that Tom's face was blanched.

"What was it—a traffic cop or a tall building?" quipped Blake, trying to make his voice sound casual.

"Almost clipped a peak," Tom replied, swallowing hard. To avoid further risk, he continued his steep climb for several thousand feet. Then he throttled down the horizontal power, so that the ship nosed through the fog at a snail's pace.

Tom snapped on the intercom and spoke to the radioman. "We're almost there, I think. Tell Hanson to listen for the sound of our engines. Soon as he hears us, ask him to shoot up a couple of signal flares for a landing marker."

"Roger!"

*It was not long before a shower*

It was not long before a shower of sparks burst into view about a hundred yards to starboard. A moment later came another.

"Okay! We've got the spot!" Tom spoke into the mike.

Banking sharply, he wheeled the plane around to the position indicated, then shut off all horizontal power. For a moment the ship hung suspended in the fog, like a gigantic toy in a frosted shopwindow.

As Tom eased off the jet lifters, the plane began to sink earthward, settling on a snow-covered rock shelf of ground.

The main door of the *Sky Queen* slid open and

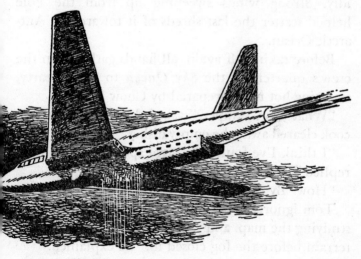

*of sparks burst into view*

the occupants jumped to the ground, clad in their electrically heated parkas. There to greet them were Hanson and his two crewmen.

"Let's see how badly your undercarriage is damaged," Tom said, after they had clasped hands.

He inspected the jet's landing gear and called for the necessary replacement parts from the supplies carried aboard the *Sky Queen*. Then the young inventor embarked on the repair job, with the help of his flight engineer.

It was a lengthy and grueling task, working with gloved hands in the bitter Antarctic cold. But by the time repairs were completed, the fog was lifting rapidly. Strong winds sweeping up from the Pole helped scatter the last shreds of it toward the Antarctic Ocean.

Before taking off again, all hands gathered in the crew's quarters of the *Sky Queen* to eat a hearty, steaming-hot meal prepared by Chow Winkler.

"What now, skipper?" asked Arv Hanson, as the cook cleared away the empty dishes.

"I think I've found the right spot for our camp," replied Tom.

"How? By crystal ball?" Voorhees sneered.

Tom ignored the gibe. "I picked it out partly by studying the map, and partly from what I saw of the terrain before the fog closed in," he explained.

Hanson followed his skipper up to the pilot's compartment where Tom pointed out the exact spot on the chart. Then, leaning close, the engineer said quietly:

"That guy Voorhees is getting to be quite a pain, isn't he?"

"As a scientist he knows his stuff," Tom commented with a shrug. "That's all I care about."

When Hanson's ship was ready, he signaled Tom. The *Sky Queen* took off first, to lead the way, followed by the cargo jet. Once they were air-borne, Chow made his way up to the pilot's compartment, where Blake and Dr. Faber had joined Tom.

"Got tired slingin' pans down in the galley," he told his young boss, "so I figgered I'd come up here an' see what you hombres was up to."

"We're trying to figure out a riddle," Blake said, giving Tom a wink. "Chow, there's one place on earth where you'd face north, no matter what direction you turned. Do you know where that is?"

The likable cook scratched his head as Tom grinned. "I'd say deep in the heart o' Texas!"

Everyone laughed heartily and Blake said, "No. Right here at the South Pole!"

"You mean every direction is up? That's more'n I kin take, podners! I'm going back to my pots an' pans."

Not long afterward, the two planes landed at the spot which Tom had chosen for the campsite. Geophones were immediately set up for a depth sounding. While an electric detonator was being hooked up to set off a charge of dynamite planted beneath the snow, Chow strolled over to watch the proceedings.

"What in thunderation you doin' now, son?" he asked Tom.

"I want to find out what's under all this ice and snow," the young inventor explained. "If the ice is resting on solid rock, we'll get only one echo from the dynamite blast. But if we're over water, we'll get two."

"Oh, I get it," Chow said importantly. "One if by land an' two if by sea!"

"Wow!" Tom exclaimed and whistled.

The test proved that they were on a rock base, suitable for drilling. By measuring the time lapse between blast and echo, Tom found that the thickness of the ice and snow was three hundred feet.

As Tom and the crew electrician were dismantling the geophone connections, the radioman from the *Sky Queen* ran up to them.

"Just picked up a message from Bud Barclay!" he reported. "The other two cargo jets are on their way!"

Tom gave a whoop of triumph. "It means that the government has okayed the expedition, after all!" Turning to the radioman, he asked, "Did you tell them our position?"

"Yes, sir. Hanson gave full instructions for getting here."

"Great!" Tom said enthusiastically. "The expedition is on!"

Before unloading either ship, however, Tom decided to make a reconnaissance flight and check on the area where they had sighted the huskies. The *Sky Queen* took off, swooping low over the icy wastes, but there was no sign of any living thing.

Just as Tom turned the plane around and was about to head back, Blake shouted, "Down there!" He pointed. "I can see something dark moving against the snow!"

Instantly Tom snatched up his own binoculars, but he got only a fleeting view before the dark object disappeared. It looked like a husky.

"It was a dog, all right!" Blake insisted. "I'm sure of that!"

Tom agreed. "Looks as if Bronich and his gang have holed in and one of their huskies broke loose momentarily."

Just then the intercom buzzed and the radioman informed Tom that his father was calling from Shopton. The young inventor flipped a switch to cut in on the short-wave radio circuit.

"Hi, Dad!" he exclaimed as his father's voice came through. "How's everything?"

"First rate. Just thought you might like to hear about that FBI report."

"You bet I would!"

"Your hunch was right, son. Many of the people who sent in that flood of complaints turned out to be known subversives. That's why the government gave the green light for your expedition!"

Tom told him about the radio message from Bud, and about finding Bronich's campsite. He also suggested that his father contact the foreign government which claimed ownership of that area, and tell them a Kranjovian agent had established a base there.

"It's too late to keep Bronich from using our blueprints," Tom concluded, "but maybe we can stop him from drilling!"

Shortly after father and son had signed off, the *Sky Queen* landed at the American camp. Several hours later the two cargo jets arrived from the States. Bud was piloting the one which carried Colonel Eagle Friend and the dogs, while Hank Sterling was at the controls of the other, accompanied by Dr. MacGregor, a slight, sandy-haired man with a trim mustache and an air of quiet competence.

Tom immediately put all hands to work building a series of mammoth ice caves lined with asbestalon for housing the planes, stores, and equipment.

With the men divided into shifts, work continued around the clock. Twenty-four hours after Bud's arrival, the job was nearly completed. Chow was just about to serve a hot meal to the off-going shift when an excited crewman ran up to Tom, shouting:

"There's a plane coming! I just picked it up on the radar! Looks like a heavy bomber!"

All work stopped as the men came dashing up to hear the news. Bud looked at Tom in dismay.

"Bronich!" he gasped.

There was no time for speculation. Tom already had assigned each crewman to a special post in case of emergencies. Now he barked an order:

*"All hands to stations! Stand by to repel attack!"*

CHAPTER 18

SNEAK RAID

AS THE MEN RACED to their emergency posts, they heard the drone of the approaching plane. An instant later the strange ship arrowed down out of the brooding gray skies. It was a jet bomber!

As the plane swooped low over the camp, the bomb-bay doors flashed open and a shiny object plunged earthward.

"A bomb!" Chow cried out. Shutting his eyes tight, he clamped both hands over his ears. But the expected blast never came. The shiny object merely plummeted into the snow.

Then the enemy plane zoomed upward and whined away over the mountains.

Tom waited a full two minutes to make sure the plane would not return. Then he emerged from his snow-cave laboratory, shouting and fanning his arms back and forth in a signal of "All clear!"

154

Everyone made a dash toward the object in the snow. But Tom warned them back until he had time to inspect it and make sure that it contained no booby trap or delayed explosive.

He soon discovered that the shiny object was merely a tin can, weighted with rocks and containing a written message. The others gathered around as Tom read it aloud:

> TOM SWIFT:
> THE U.S. HAS NO RIGHT IN THIS PART OF
> THE ANTARCTIC. ABANDON YOUR BASE
> AT ONCE OR WE WILL ATTACK!

Angry murmurs arose from the crewmen. Chow exploded with indignation. "Why, them jet-propelled polecats!" he raged. "Sounds like they're fixin' to start a war at the South Pole!"

"If they want trouble, they can have it," said Tom grimly. "But first we'll call their bluff."

The young inventor hastily wrote out a message, then passed it around for the others to read. It said:

> TO IVOR BRONICH AND THE KRANJOVIAN
> INVADERS:
> WE ARE HERE TO STAY. I WARN YOU THAT
> IF YOU BOTHER US, OR MAKE USE OF THE
> INVENTION WHICH YOU STOLE FROM ME,
> YOU WILL ANSWER TO THE UNITED
> STATES GOVERNMENT.
> TOM SWIFT JR.

"And just how do you plan to deliver this message, may I ask?" inquired Voorhees with scorn in his voice.

"The same way they delivered theirs—by plane."

"Let me take it!" Bud demanded eagerly.

"It's all yours!" Tom agreed.

Quickly one of the cargo jets was rolled out of its ice-dome hangar, and the young flier took off. Tom and the others gathered in the radio shack to maintain contact with Bud during the flight.

The minutes ticked by slowly as they waited. Finally Bud's voice came crackling over the loudspeaker.

"Barclay to American base. . . . Now approaching enemy camp. . . . They're scurrying around like crazy down there! . . . Guess they didn't expect an answer so soon. . . . Their bomber in plain sight on the ground. . . . Looks as if it just landed a few moments ago."

The listeners heard Bud chuckle to himself. Then he added, "Man, what I wouldn't give for a hatchful of bombs right now—even one little teeny one!"

Tom grabbed the mike. "Remember what I told you, Bud! Don't go asking for trouble!"

"You're the boss, skipper!" There was a brief silence, then Bud's voice came through again, "Message on target! . . . Over!"

When Bud returned and circled in for a perfect landing, the men swarmed around to congratulate him as he climbed out of the cargo jet. There were questions and laughter, and jokes cracked at the expense of the startled Kranjovians.

Tom, however, was already thinking about his next move. He spoke to Bud, Arv Hanson, and Hank Sterling. "From now on, we'd better take no chances. We'll keep a man on the radarscope at all times, and make a reconnaissance flight every few hours. We four are the only pilots in the group, so we'll rotate the flights among us."

An air of tension settled over the camp as work continued in building and organizing the base. Twenty-four hours went by. Still there was no sign of a return visit from the Kranjovians.

"Apparently Bronich's threat was just what I had suspected—a bluff!" Tom mused. Nevertheless, he was worried, realizing that he was engaged in a deadly race with a ruthless opponent.

Redoubling his efforts, Tom worked at a furious pace. Besides taking his turn on the regular patrol flights, he hurried back and forth, supervising the work of the entire expedition.

"Son, don't you think you'd better slack down a bit?" Chow said. "After all, you ain't the only cowpoke on this range."

"I can't slow down," Tom replied. "Not till we strike that molten iron and make sure Bronich can't ruin our plans!"

With the expedition snugly housed against the

Antarctic cold, Tom next turned his attention to the job of preparing for the drilling. As the first step, he called the entire crew of technicians into his snow-cave laboratory, which was to serve as the central control post for his atomic earth blaster.

"Here's what our operating layout will look like," he announced, pointing to a large wall chart. "There'll be three listening posts set up around the pit dug by the blaster. The posts will be located, like the points of a triangle, about five miles apart."

"What's the purpose of the listening posts?" asked Bud.

Tom explained that sonic vibrators on the atomic earth blaster would send out vibrations, which, in turn, would be picked up by listening devices at each post.

"The data collected by these listening devices," Tom explained, "will be fed to this electronic brain here in my lab. The brain will then figure out the exact position of the blaster inside the earth at any given time."

Chow, who was standing behind the group of technicians, listened with a strained, intense look. Suddenly he spoke up, "Tom," he said, "suppose that there giant bug goes loco an' starts borin' off in the wrong direction. How you gonna ride herd on the doggone thing?"

"Good question," Tom replied, smiling. "This

gadget here will do the trick." He pointed to a device near the electronic brain. "It's a sonic vibrator, like the ones on the blaster. Only this one will send instructions down to the blaster instead of pulsing signals up to us."

With a wise look, Chow nodded approval.

Tom said that the job of setting up the listening posts would begin immediately. The necessary building material and equipment would be hauled to each location by dog team and snowmobile.

A short time later the first team of technicians set out from the base. In the lead was the snowmobile, plowing a trail through the crusted snow with its blunt nose and wide caterpillar treads. Behind came the dog-team freight sled, guided by Colonel Eagle Friend and loaded down with additional supplies and equipment.

Work went ahead rapidly on the three listening posts. In the one nearest the digging site, Voorhees installed special temperature recorders. These would pick up readings from delicate thermal-measuring devices inside the blaster, and thus show the earth's temperature at every point as the blaster went down deeper and deeper.

Before launching the blaster, Tom double-checked his depth soundings. He wanted to make sure how soon he could expect to hit solid rock.

Just as the geophones were being connected, a siren screeched. This was the alarm signal from the radarman.

"It's another air raid!" Blake shouted, as all hands made a dash for their emergency stations.

A moment later the same jet bomber that had buzzed the camp before came roaring down out of the skies. But again it passed over harmlessly—this time without even dropping a message.

Puzzled and somewhat worried, Tom gave the all-clear signal for his aides to return to work. They had hardly resumed their tasks, however, when once again the siren shrieked.

Dropping their tools, the men started to run for cover. But there was no time to reach safety. A blurred object streaked across the sky and headed directly for the camp.

"A guided missile!" Bud yelled. "It's going to hit us!"

## CHAPTER 19

## DISASTER STRIKES

A SPLIT SECOND LATER the missile struck— a clean hit on the ice cave housing the spare blaster!

A deafening explosion rocked the area and the ice cave flew apart in a burst of smoke and flame! Metal fragments were sprayed over the entire camp.

Furious and sickened by the sudden blow, Tom could hardly speak. He stood clenching his fists and gritting his teeth as he fought to master the feelings of rage and despair that swept over him.

With the spare blaster gone, everything hinged on the successful operation of the single atomic drill. If this blaster were pinned or crushed while digging the shaft, the entire expedition would be a failure. Swift Enterprises and the Swift Construction Company would be ruined!

"What will we do now?" asked Dr. Faber gravely, as Tom's men gathered around.

"Give those Kranjovians a taste of their own medicine!" Tom turned to his flight crewmen. "Roll the *Sky Queen* out of her hangar and get her ready for immediate take-off!"

The men were exultant at the news that Tom was about to strike back at the enemy. Colonel Eagle Friend and some of the others begged for a chance to accompany him on the flight. But Tom decided to limit his crew to one man—his husky copilot, Bud Barclay.

As the great silver ship streaked through the polar sky en route to the enemy camp, Tom's nerves were calm and steady.

"Coming on target!" shouted Bud. Far below, they could see the antlike forms of men. The tail end of the enemy's jet bomber was just disappearing inside its own ice-dome hangar.

Jamming the stick forward, Tom sent the *Sky Queen* into a screaming dive. As the mammoth ship plunged earthward like a silver thunderbolt, the Kranjovians scattered in wild panic.

"We've scared 'em. Now we'll melt 'em," Tom said, guiding the plane out of the dive and soaring skyward.

Reducing the forward thrust, Tom cut loose with a full blast of power from the jet lifters, raking the camp from one end to the other! The heat plowed a deep furrow in the snow, melting and crumpling the roofs of several ice-cave dwellings.

But this time the Kranjovians were ready. Throwing the camouflage off their gun placements, they brought the long, deadly muzzles of their ack-ack batteries wheeling into action.

As the great ship zoomed over the camp, the guns began to spit and the air blossomed with a hail of shells. But even though many whizzed perilously close to the *Sky Queen,* not one of the shells exploded!

Bud was beside himself with glee as he peered down at the enemy gunners through binoculars.

"You should see 'em, Tom!" he said. "They're going crazy! They can't figure out why the proximity fuses on the shells aren't going off!"

"Wonderful stuff, this Tomasite!" The young inventor chuckled. The special plastic coating completely covered the *Sky Queen* and insulated it from magnetic effects.

On the next run, the Kranjovians tried again to down the avenging plane. Again they failed completely.

"Once more for good luck!" Tom said, as he brought the ship around for a final run over the target. This time, the enemy gunners gave up in despair and scattered for cover.

"Brother, I'll bet you scared those guys out of a year's growth!" gasped Bud, weak with laughter, as the *Sky Queen* roared up and away from the Kranjovian camp.

But both Tom and Bud knew that a single scare, however effective, would not long deter the efforts of Bronich and his henchmen to wipe out the Swift expedition. As soon as the boys arrived back at camp, Tom called a meeting to report what had happened. All except Voorhees cheered Tom's success, after which Bud broached the idea of invading the enemy base and overpowering the Kranjovians.

"Until we put them out of action, once and for all," the copilot said, "we can never rest easy! At any time they may launch another sneak attack!"

Tom disagreed, warning of the danger of a possible global war as the result. It was finally decided to wait until word arrived from Mr. Swift as to whether or not Bronich had a right to operate in that part of the Antarctic. Meanwhile, Tom laid out further defense plans, then resumed his job of checking depth soundings. The geophones were set up and a charge of dynamite was touched off deep beneath the snow.

An amplifying recording device photographed the sound waves of the explosion as they were picked up over the geophones. As he studied the results Tom frowned, then a look of dismay crossed his face.

"Something wrong, chum?" Bud asked.

"Plenty! According to our previous soundings, we were based on solid rock. Now we're getting a double echo—which means we're over water."

"Impossible!" Bud insisted.

Quickly Tom checked several other points about the camp. The government scientists and several of the crewmen gathered around to watch. In every case, the test showed the same results!

"I don't get it," said Bud with a puzzled look. "If your first soundings showed rock, how could it change to water?"

"Very simple, I'm afraid," Tom replied. "The ice on which our camp is resting must have shifted during the last few days."

"You're right, Tom," Dr. Faber agreed. "That means we're now on a floating ice shelf which could break apart at any moment!"

Disheartened, the members of the expedition looked at each other until Bud spoke again.

"What's our next move?" he asked.

"Looks as if we'll have to move southward, nearer the Pole, perhaps along the foot of the Queen Maud Mountains. Then we can be sure of drilling into solid rock."

Voorhees' lip curled in a sneer.

"Don't you think it's about time you started facing the facts?" he inquired with a nasty edge to his voice.

Tom eyed him coolly. "Such as?"

"Such as the fact that you've bungled this expedition from the word go!"

Bud shoved his way forward to stand face to face with Voorhees. "Maybe you'd like to back up that statement, Hal," he suggested, knowing the nickname would irritate Voorhees. "Tell us exactly *how* Tom has bungled this expedition."

"I should think that would be obvious, even to you," Voorhees jeered. "While we've been wasting valuable time setting up a base here—on a site, by the way, which was chosen personally by young Mr. Swift—Bronich has probably picked the ideal spot for drilling!"

"And of course you could have handled things much better?" Bud challenged.

"I certainly couldn't have handled them any worse!"

"Then try handling this!"

Bud's fist shot out in a punch that sent Voorhees sprawling in the snow!

# CHAPTER 20

# A WHALE CHARGES

THE KNOCKDOWN infuriated Voorhees. Crimson with rage, he picked himself up and charged.

Bud met him with a jarring left to the jaw, followed by a hard right to the pit of the stomach. Voorhees' knees buckled, but he quickly recovered. A moment later the opponents were trading punches wildly in a toe-to-toe slugging match, hindered greatly by their heavy clothing.

The clash had caught Tom by surprise. But before any serious harm could be done, he flung himself between the fighters and pushed them apart.

"Now shake hands—both of you!" Tom ordered. "And don't give me any argument. We've got too big a job ahead of us to waste any energy brawling!"

The commanding ring in his voice produced

instant results. Somewhat shamefacedly, Bud and Voorhees shook hands.

"Perhaps it would be better to move after all," Voorhees conceded sullenly. "My own thermal measurements will be more stable if they're made on solid rock."

During the next two days, Tom scouted a large area to the south, taking numerous soundings with the geophones. Finally he found what seemed to be an ideal spot for drilling.

In the days that followed, everyone worked steadily at the job of shifting the base camp and setting up new listening posts.

The last link in the preparations, prior to launching the blaster, was the digging of an enormous artificial "lake" in the ice. Then the lake would be drained, in order to provide an immense cup in which to capture the molten iron as it spouted up from the earth. Tom summoned the crewmen to his laboratory to explain this operation.

"I'll melt the ice with the jet lifters of the *Sky Queen*," he told them. "The water will then be pumped off rapidly through a large hose."

Tom gave orders for the hose to be lashed down with wire cables and the nozzle to be fixed in position with powerful clamps.

Immediately after lunch, Tom and Bud took off in the *Sky Queen*. Tom brought the big plane over the area marked out for the pool and glided to an altitude of only a few hundred feet.

Then, throttling down on the horizontal power, he began circling slowly around and around while the jet lifters poured a steady stream of heat into the snow.

Soon the artificial lake was gushing with melted snow. As the pumps picked up suction, the hose suddenly came to life. It swelled and stiffened, violent blasts of water shooting out the nozzle. Gradually, the lake was drained.

Upon returning to camp just before supper, Tom learned that the sonic devices for transmitting signals back and forth between the blaster and the listening posts were not working properly.

The engineers, however, told him that they had located the cause of the trouble and would have the mechanisms in good working order within forty-eight hours.

On the basis of this report, Tom decided to plan on launching the blaster in three days. Before going to bed, he strolled over to the radio shack to contact his father and find out if Bronich had permission to operate in the area.

The radioman was now using a code machine to scramble and unscramble messages, as a precaution against the Kranjovians learning their plans.

This time, however, as he beamed a call signal to

Shopton, the speaker could pick up nothing but violent, blasting static. After repeated attempts to get through, the radioman finally gave up.

"Must be some violent electrical storms going on between here and the States," he reported.

"Either that, or Bronich is jamming our signals!" returned Tom grimly. As he made his way back to his snow-cave laboratory, he met Daryl Blake and Dr. Faber. Blake, excited as a schoolboy, invited Tom to the botany lab on the *Sky Queen*.

"Now, my friends," announced the red-haired scientist as Tom and Dr. Faber followed him into his workshop, "feast your eyes on this!"

With the air of a magician pulling a rabbit out of a hat, Blake produced two exhibits of lichens—a small clinging plant found at the South Pole. One specimen was frozen solidly in ice, the other was growing luxuriantly under the rays of a sun lamp.

Next, he pointed out a display of ivy and mountain pinks—some quick-frozen and some flourishing in a tray "garden."

Tom and Faber looked on fascinated as Blake continued:

"This will revolutionize horticulture and the study of plant growth! From now on, seedlings and small plants can be frozen and shipped anywhere in the world!"

"Right!" Tom exclaimed. "And not only that—

the treatment would kill off any harmful insect life that might be carried along."

Dr. Faber's eyes danced. "Think of it!" He chuckled. "A deep freezer in every florist's shop!"

When Blake had finished showing his exhibit, Tom congratulated the botanist on his success. As the three left the laboratory, Dr. Faber said, "I was wondering if you'd care to accompany me tomorrow on a short field trip to study the Antarctic wildlife? I'm particularly interested in making some observations on the behavior of penguins and whales."

"Fine!" agreed Tom, who was in the mood for some recreation. "We'll take the pontoon plane."

This was a light and useful little amphibian craft which he had substituted for the jet-lifted helicopter just before leaving Shopton.

After an eight-hour sleep and a good breakfast, Tom and Dr. Faber took off. At first the sky was clear and the mountain ridges cast blue-black shadows in the snow. Everything stood out in sharply chiseled detail. On the exposed cliff faces, red and green lichens mingled with white and gray patches against the blackish rock, creating a colorful effect.

But gradually the sky became overcast. Earth and sky seemed to meet in a ghostly, shadowless white universe with no horizons. Tom headed for the Bay of Whales, a watery indentation in the great Ross Barrier.

On a snow field at the edge of the water, where they sighted a large school of Adélie penguins, Tom came down for a landing.

The friendly, frolicking birds seemed absolutely fearless and quickly came waddling over to inspect the visitors. With their white breasts, shiny black coats, and flippers, they looked like funny little gentlemen in evening clothes.

Dr. Faber made notes and took photographs while Tom watched some of the penguins playing a game. A group would gather around a snow hill and watch solemnly while one climbed to the top. He would stand staring out to sea for a while, then another would climb up and push him off.

The newcomer, too, would stand gazing off into the distance until another penguin pushed *him* off. One by one, they took turns being "king of the castle."

Finally one of the penguins began picking up small pebbles in his beak and bringing them over to drop at Tom's feet.

"He seems to have taken quite a shine to you." Dr. Faber chuckled. "That's a sign of penguin approval. Incidentally, that's how a gentleman penguin woos the lady of his choice."

"Good night!" Tom grinned. "Let's get out of here before he tries to kiss me!"

They took off, this time cruising over the open

water hoping to sight a whale. The bay was studded with drift ice and floating icebergs. Unlike the northern variety, these Antarctic bergs were long and flat, some extending for two miles in length.

At Dr. Faber's suggestion, Tom brought the plane down on the water so they could observe some of the seals which were sliding on the ice. As Tom maneuvered the craft skillfully alongside several of the creatures, the elder scientist gave a sudden cry of alarm. Tom looked in the direction he was pointing, then gasped.

From behind a nearby iceberg, a mammoth whale had reared its enormous head and was charging directly toward them!

# CHAPTER 21

# A HAIRBREADTH ESCAPE

AS THE WHALE bore down on them, Tom opened the throttle wide, shooting the plane across the choppy gray-green waters of the bay.

In order to get close to the seals, Tom had maneuvered into an area littered with drift ice. Now his course was blocked by numerous floating white chunks.

Kicking the rudder hard, the inventor veered to the left and headed for open water, as Dr. Faber cried out:

"It's a blue whale—the biggest kind there is!" Excitedly he pulled out his pen and notebook and started writing.

Just at that moment, the whale spouted, then plunged below the surface and disappeared.

The plane was skimming along, nearing open water now, with a clear path ahead for a take-off. A stiff breeze was whipping the waves into whitecaps.

Suddenly, with a loud splash, the whale surfaced again, fifty feet directly ahead, rearing and arcing its body.

Tom gasped, "It must be a hundred feet long!"

"And weigh more than a hundred tons!" added Dr. Faber, scribbling notes furiously.

Tom gunned the engines to pick up speed for the take-off. Would they make it, or hit the whale? Tom pulled back on the stick. The pontoons cleared the water and the craft was air-borne! They had missed the whale's back by a scant three feet!

Not until they were soaring safely above the bay did the two explorers exchange glances and let out deep sighs of relief.

"Magnificent, the way you kept your head and steered us out of danger, Tom!" Dr. Faber congratulated him.

"I was too scared to do anything else!" the young inventor confessed ruefully. "You're the one who was really fearless, the way you kept taking notes."

The scientist's steel-gray eyes twinkled. "The truth is," he explained, "I had to go on writing to keep from panicking. But now look at me!"

He held out his hand and Tom saw that it was shaking like a leaf. With the sudden release of tension, both Tom and Dr. Faber burst into laughter.

On the flight back to camp, they passed numerous birds of the Antarctic. Several times Tom swooped low so Dr. Faber could examine flocks of skua gulls and snowy petrels.

As the plane regained altitude, the elder scientist noticed that Tom looked worried. "Anything wrong?" he inquired.

"I seem to be a bit off course," Tom replied. He circled left, then headed back in the direction from which they had just come. Once more he circled.

"Are we lost?" Dr. Faber asked calmly.

"I'm afraid we are. According to my computations, we should be just about over the camp. But there's no sign of it."

"Any chance of a mistake?"

"I don't think so. But wait a minute." Hastily Tom checked his navigation figures, then shook his head.

"No, the figures are okay," he added, "unless my instruments are way off. Of course, they may have been affected by terrestrial magnetism. And with this overcast, there's no hope of getting a sun sight."

Nothing was visible below but a vast expanse of white wilderness. Tom tried to line up his position on the chart by referring to some mountain peaks to the southward. But the mountains were so poorly mapped that it was impossible to get a definite fix.

The young inventor paled as a horrible thought

struck him. "A flash blizzard!" he gasped. "One may have struck the camp while we were gone and covered everything!"

With mounting worry, Tom and Dr. Faber scanned the terrain with their glasses. Just when hope seemed to ebb, two figures emerged from the snowy vastness and waved.

"Where did they come from?" Dr. Faber asked, astonished.

Tom eased the plane down lower for a closer look through the binoculars, then gave a shout of relief. "They're Bud and Hanson!"

Minutes later, he landed the plane and taxied to a halt near several great *sastrugi*—wind-blown drifts of snow. Bud and Hanson ran up to greet them.

"For Pete's sake, what happened to the camp?" asked Tom anxiously. In reply, Bud stuck his arm into one of the big snowdrifts, then tugged upward, displaying a corner of tarpaulin covered with snow.

"There's your answer, chum," Bud said. "Stick your head under that tarp and you'll find the lab. Every other building on the base is camouflaged the same way."

"Great idea," Tom said, "but you might have told a fellow about it."

"I didn't have time," Bud said, "on account of the attack."

"Another one?"

"And how! Sent their jet bomber over again. The pilot dropped a stick of bombs on us. Luckily, they all landed off the target, so no one was hurt."

Hanson spoke up. "Tom, we figured it would be wise to camouflage the camp, in case the plane came back."

While Tom was talking with Bud and Hanson, the other members of the expedition emerged from their hiding places in the camouflage snowdrifts. They gathered around to add their own angry remarks to the report of the Kranjovian bombing attack.

"I was so doggone mad," Bud stormed, "that I almost took off in the *Sky Queen* and blasted 'em from here to the North Pole! But Hal Voorhees and some of the others persuaded me to wait for you."

"I'm glad you did," said Tom thoughtfully. "It looks as if it's time to take definite action. This situation has gone far enough!"

Quickly he ordered the *Sky Queen* to be hauled out of its hangar. Soon the great ship was streaking toward the enemy base. Tom was seated at the controls, with Bud Barclay in the copilot's seat beside him.

As they came in sight of the Kranjovian base, they saw a cluster of men swarming around something at the southern edge of the camp.

"What's going on down there?" Bud said.

"We'll soon find out," Tom replied. Easing off the jet lifters, he sent the *Sky Queen* swooping down over the heads of the Kranjovians. As they scattered, Bud gave an excited cry:

"Look! They're launching an earth blaster!"

# CHAPTER 22

# PRISONER OF WAR

"JUMPIN' JETS! The Kranjovians have an earth blaster too!" Bud shouted.

"It's almost identical to mine," Tom said, looking down at a steel-girdered platform. On it the inventor saw a long, gleaming cylinder with protruding electrodes at the nose! The machine was poised for launching!

"Those sneak thieves must have made it from your blueprints!" Bud exclaimed. "Let's go down there right now and blast the daylights out of 'em!"

The young inventor shook his head thoughtfully as he circled above the camp. "No, I'm afraid that's not the answer," he said. "Suppose Bronich is operating with permission from the country which claims this part of the Antarctic. If we destroy his camp, that country might consider it an act of war."

"But where does that leave us?" Bud grumbled.

Tom thought for a moment. "I'll try to get through to Shopton and see if Dad has any information for us yet. Then we can decide what to do."

As Bud took over the controls, Tom stepped aft to the radio compartment and switched on the short-wave transmitter. As soon as the set was warmed up, he began beaming a code signal to Shopton. The only result was loud, sputtering static.

Bud flashed Tom a questioning look as the young inventor resumed his seat in the pilot's compartment.

"Any luck?"

"No. Sounds as if they're still jamming the air waves."

"Okay. So what happens now, jet boy?"

"The only thing left is to try to arrange a truce and talk with Bronich in person." Tom strode to the radio cabin and returned about fifteen minutes later.

"What's the deal?" the copilot asked.

"Bronich agrees," Tom said tersely. "Let's take her down."

Like a great silver bird, the *Sky Queen* swooped for a landing in the snow. As Tom unbuckled his seat belt and prepared to leave the plane, Bud moved to accompany him. But Tom motioned him back.

"You'd better stay here, pal. There may be trouble. I want you to keep the plane ready for an instant take-off, in case Bronich decides not to respect the truce."

Bud watched uneasily through the window of the pilot's compartment as his friend emerged from the plane and advanced toward the Kranjovians. Clad in heavy furs, they were drawn together in a group to meet him. The men were rough-looking and unshaven. At the head of the group was a tall, gaunt figure in a black bearskin parka. Tom recognized him instantly as Ivor Bronich.

"Well, what is it you want?" snarled the Kranjovian spy in his thick accent.

"I want to keep you out of trouble if I can," Tom said.

"Trouble? Ha! It is you who are in trouble, my friend, not I," Bronich said, laughing.

Tom ignored the gibe. "I don't believe you have any right to be operating here," Tom said, but added quickly, "However, if you do have, why can't we go about our experiments peacefully?"

The young inventor was mentally sparring for time. The longer he could delay Bronich from using the usurped earth blaster, the better were the chances of having the subversives captured.

"You ask for peace?" Bronich stormed. "You who have stolen the earth blaster from Kranjovia?"

Anger surged through Tom. "Who stole what?"

"You stole our idea," Bronich said. "Kranjovian engineers developed this ten years ago!"

"Why didn't you make use of it?"

"We were improving on it for our glorious country," Bronich replied.

"Your facts are slightly inaccurate," Tom said, trying hard to control his temper. "You stole the blueprints from me."

At this Bronich turned to view his cohorts, an ugly sneer on his face. Pointing to Tom, he shouted:

"Liar!"

Impulsively Tom lashed out and hit the spy hard on the mouth, cutting his lower lip. But before he could land another blow, the Kranjovians had overpowered him.

"You will live to regret this!" Bronich hissed.

In the cabin of the *Sky Queen*, Bud had seen everything that happened and he realized that by himself it was hopeless to try to free Tom from the enemy.

"But maybe there's another way!" Bud muttered. He gave a blast of power to the jet lifters and the *Sky Queen* zoomed up, then soared away as though fleeing from the Kranjovian camp.

Suddenly he banked the plane sharply and sent it roaring back straight at the enemy! He was hoping to catch Bronich and his men by surprise. But the

Kranjovian agent had spotted Bud's maneuver. Before Bud could let go with a searing blast from the jet lifters, Bronich's men had dragged Tom straight into the path of the oncoming plane.

They were using the young inventor as a human shield! Bud fumed with helpless rage. But there was nothing he could do except shut off the jet lifters and wing harmlessly over the heads of the enemy. He refused to give up, however. Again and again, he made lightning passes at the Kranjovians, coming at them from every direction.

But each time Bronich's men thwarted Bud's attack by shoving Tom directly in his line of fire.

Finally the copilot realized there was only one way to save his friend and that was to get help. Roaring upward in a steep climb, he sent the *Sky Queen* streaking homeward toward the American camp.

Watching the great plane disappear in the distance, Bronich broke into loud, snorting laughter.

"So! Your friend runs away, like typical Yankee dog, with his tail between his legs!" Bronich turned mockingly to Tom. "And now, since you violated our truce, you will stay and become one of us!"

"If you think I'm going to help you, you've got another think coming!" Tom said defiantly.

Bronich sneered, "Never fear, my young friend. We Kranjovians have many ways to bend a man to our will. If and when the time comes that we should need your scientific help in operating this so-called earth blaster, I assure you that you will render assistance gladly."

Tom glared at him. "Then you admit it's a copy of my machine?"

"Of course! Why not? I see no further need for evasion." Bronich chuckled. "I will also admit something more. We were planning to destroy your American base tomorrow. But, in view of the present turn of events, why should we delay? I will give orders for the bombing planes and rockets to be launched at once!"

Although sick with horror at the impending peril, Tom was thinking fast. As Bronich began barking out commands to his men, the young inventor suddenly spoke up.

"Wait a minute! Let's see your blaster in operation. How do I know this whole setup isn't just a big bluff?"

Bronich considered for a moment, eying Tom narrowly. Finally he said, "Very well. We shall start the machine and you may watch. Meanwhile, my men will be attacking and destroying your friends!"

All the time, Tom had been studying the setup. Somehow he must warn his friends! As he walked toward the launching platform with Bronich and the crew, he was thinking:

"The controls—if I can just get at the controls, maybe I can foul up the blaster and upset the camp long enough to make a getaway!"

# CHAPTER 23

# SHOWDOWN BATTLE

AS BUD LANDED the *Sky Queen* at the American camp, the scientists and crewmen swarmed out of their ice caves to hear what had happened. When the copilot climbed out of the plane alone, they realized that something was wrong.

"Where's Tom?" shouted Arvid Hanson anxiously.

When Bud told them the bad news, the men became fighting mad.

"Them sneakin' double-dyed polecats!" stormed Chow Winkler. "We oughta rope an' hog-tie every last one of 'em an' feed 'em to the whales!"

"They'll get what's coming to them!" vowed Hank Sterling. "Right now, it's Tom we must worry about!"

"We'd better move fast," Bud said. "Let's all go in the *Sky Queen*. We can force them to release Tom

186

by threatening to wipe out their base if they refuse!"

By common consent, Bud took charge of the preparations, with Hank Sterling as second in command. A supply of tear-gas guns and tear-gas bombs—the only weapons ever carried by a Swift expedition—were lugged out of one of the ice caves and loaded on board the plane.

Just as the men were being mustered and organized, the radioman came running up. "There's a call coming through from Shopton!" he reported. "I think it's Mr. Swift Sr."

"I'll take it," said Bud. But he dreaded the thought of breaking the news about Tom's capture.

In the communications cave he waited as the radioman fed the signal into the unscrambling device. Soon the voice of Tom's father came over the speaker:

"Good news, son! I've contacted the foreign government which claims the part of the Antarctic where Bronich has set up his base. They've given him no permission to tap the mineral resources of their territory! They're now sending planes and men to take the necessary police action. But, in the meantime, they request that you folks do all you can to stop him! . . . Over."

At the last moment Bud could not bear to burden the elder scientist with worry over his son's plight. He spoke into the mike:

"American base to Shopton. . . . This is Bud

Barclay speaking. . . . Tom's not here just now, Mr. Swift, but I'll get your message to him as soon as possible!"

Bud signed off and hurried back to the *Sky Queen,* where his "troops" were waiting to embark. He was reporting the news from Shopton when the shrill whine of the air-raid siren sounded over the camp!

The men scattered for cover. Seconds later the jet bomber came swooping down. But there was no attack. Instead of bombs, another weighted tin can was dropped from the plane. Bud ran to pluck out the message and read it aloud:

> TO THE AMERICAN EXPEDITION: WE ARE HOLDING TOM SWIFT AS A HOSTAGE. DO NOT TRY TO ATTACK OUR CAMP OR HE WILL SUFFER THE CONSEQUENCES!

The men's faces showed dismay. Even Bud was nonplused for a moment by the unexpected threat. But a surge of anger and indignation quickly stiffened his resolve.

"We can't let them bluff us this way! Tom's in danger whether we attack or not! And it's a cinch they'll never let him go free unless we rescue him!"

"Yo're dad-blamed right they won't!" Chow Winkler chimed in. "There's only one kind o' language them hoot owls understand, an' it's time we started talkin' it!"

Most of the men were quickly won over to this point of view. But Voorhees objected.

"You're asking us to take full responsibility for whatever happens to Tom Swift. If an armed force is on its way here by plane, why not wait and let them handle the situation?"

Bud glared at him. "That's about what I expected from you, Hal!"

The argument flared back and forth, with two or three of the crewmen supporting Voorhees. Finally a compromise was reached. Voorhees' group agreed to stay and guard the camp, while Bud led the assault force to rescue Tom.

Presently the *Sky Queen* took off on its dangerous mission. When they came in sight of the Kranjovian camp, it was plain that the enemy was prepared for an attack. Two gun crews were on guard against intruders. Otherwise, there was no one in sight.

As the *Sky Queen* swooped down, the Kranjovian gunners sent up a hail of flack. But as before, the shells glanced harmlessly past the *Sky Queen* and failed to explode.

Bud opened up with the jet lifters and raked the camp from end to end with blasts of flame. Realizing their own weapons were useless, the enemy gunners fled in panic, disappearing into a large ice cave.

"Must be their main fort," observed Hank Sterling.

"Why not fly over it and blast it to a puddle!" Daryl Blake suggested.

"Tom may be in there," Bud snapped tensely. "We'll have to attack on the ground and try to drive them out into the open!"

Landing the plane, Bud taxied the big ship up close to the cave entrance. A rifle barrel protruding at each corner showed the presence of armed sentries.

"What now, general?" asked Arv Hanson. "Do we pile out?"

"Not yet. First we'll take care of those guards!"

Under Hank Sterling's direction, tear-gas weapons and gas masks were issued to all hands. Meanwhile, the guards, sensing that an attack was being readied, started firing nervously at the plane.

Bud opened one of the cargo hatches a few inches and poked out the muzzle of a tear-gas gun. Drawing a bead on a point near one of the guards, he fired.

As the shell splattered against the wall of the cave, the guard was engulfed in a fuming spray of gas. Then Bud fired at a point near the other man, and he, too, was drenched with a burst of tear gas.

Clawing at their eyes and gasping for air, the Kranjovian sentinels threw down their rifles and came stumbling out of the cave to sprawl headlong in the snow.

"All right, let's go!" Bud shouted. "But remember—stay out of the line of fire from the cave!"

Throwing the doors of the cargo hatch wide open, the Americans leaped from the plane, captured the guards, and marched them a safe distance from the scene of action.

Then Bud gave the signal for an all-out attack. Instantly his men began hurling bombs and lobbing tear-gas cartridges into the cave.

In order to fight back, the Kranjovians had to crawl to the entrance. But when they did, they were met by a curtain of stinging, choking gas.

"Only a question of time now," murmured Dr. Faber, during a lull in the fire. "Soon the whole cave will be full of gas."

A few moments later the Kranjovians came running, lurching, and staggering out of their icy fortress with tears streaming down their faces.

As they choked and sputtered, most of them were in no condition to offer any resistance. But a few still showed signs of fight.

One burly, black-bearded Kranjovian tried to batter his way to freedom, but was promptly knocked out by a sledge-hammer blow from Colonel Eagle Friend's fist.

Firing wildly with an automatic pistol, Bronich tried to shoot his way clear. But as soon as the gun was empty, Bud went after him.

Grabbing Bronich by the hood of his parka, Bud swung him around. The treacherous spy dropped his gun and jerked out a knife. Before he could use it, however, Bud staggered him with a smashing right to the jaw, kicked the knife out of his hand, and dragged him back to where the other prisoners were lined up.

Arvid Hanson greeted Bud with an anxious cry. "Tom's not in the cave!"

"What!"

Shoving Bronich toward Hank Sterling to be handcuffed, Bud readjusted his gas mask and plunged into the cave. Hanson was right—Tom was nowhere inside!

When Bud emerged, he ordered a search made of all the other caves on the base. There was no trace of the young inventor anywhere!

Angrily Bud began firing questions at the prisoners. But they merely stared back in sullen silence and refused to say a word about Tom's fate.

The Americans looked at each other in grim despair, afraid to voice the thought that was uppermost in all their minds.

*Had Tom Swift been killed?*

**CHAPTER 24**

# A VOLCANIC ERUPTION

"COME ON, let's snap out of it!" Bud shouted. "Tom must be around here somewhere!"

"Why, brand my snowshoes, o' course he is!" asserted Chow gruffly. "Don't you figger a smart buckeroo like Tom knows how to take care o' himself?"

"Wait a minute!" Bud cried. "I just had an idea!" He asked if anyone had noticed a sled or huskies anywhere around the Kranjovians' camp. No one had.

"Don't you see?" he went on. "We know they had a team, 'cause that's how Tom spotted the camp to begin with. But now the dogs are gone. So that means either Tom made a getaway in the sled, or else one of Bronich's men must have carried him off on it!"

"It figures, all right," agreed Hank Sterling cautiously. "But how do we find him?"

Hastily Bud formulated plans for a search party. He himself would set out in Bronich's snowmobile, accompanied by Blake and Dr. Faber. Meanwhile, Hank Sterling would go aloft in the *Sky Queen*, with Chow and Colonel Eagle Friend as spotters, and scout the whole surrounding area. The other members of the party would stay behind to guard the prisoners.

Twenty mintues later, as Bud and his companions were plowing along through the mountain foothills, Hank Sterling's voice crackled over the walkie-talkie:

"I think I've found him! There's a sled and dog team heading toward our camp! Keep your eyes peeled for the *Sky Queen* and I'll point you in the right direction!"

Gunning the snowmobile at top speed and following Hank's radioed instructions, Bud finally overtook the driver of the sled.

*It was Tom Swift!*

"Genius boy!" yelled Bud, as they pounded each other joyfully. Dr. Faber, Blake, and Bud quickly brought Tom up to date on all the news, and described the capture of the Kranjovians.

"Great!" Tom exclaimed. "Now there's nothing more to hold us back! We'll put our earth blaster to work immediately."

"Wait a minute, Tom," put in Blake. "You still haven't told us how you escaped!"

"It was simple," Tom said, grinning. "I broke away from the guards, ran into their control cave, and deactivated their blaster just when Bronich was all set to launch it. In the confusion that followed I borrowed their dogs and cleared out!"

Bud shook his head in mock dejection. "Next time you get captured," he said, "we'll rescue the villains and let you thumb a ride home by yourself!"

On the way back to the Kranjovian camp, Tom realized that he could not begin his own digging operations until all his men were free from guard duty. He decided to remain at the enemy base till the prisoners were picked up.

While waiting, Tom quizzed several of the Kranjovian crewmen who were now willing to co-operate. One of them turned out to be Podski, Bronich's right-hand man. He supplied the answers to a number of the young inventor's questions. Podski exonerated the Excelsis Club, but confessed that the headwaiter, a Kranjovian, had discovered the lakeside passageway and had arranged for the spy ring to meet secretly at the club.

He revealed that the Kranjovian transmitter had been jamming the air waves, just as Tom had suspected. Also, that it was Bronich who had sabotaged the alarm system at the Swift home—and that same night had overheard Tom's whole discussion about tapping iron at the South Pole!

Bronich, it turned out, was also responsible for placing the bombs in the tunnel through Pine Hill.

"So that clears Picken completely," Tom remarked to Bud.

At last, almost twenty-four hours after Tom's rescue, a flight of military planes arrived from the country which claimed the territory invaded by Bronich.

The officer in charge, Colonel Jardin, was immediately taken to the cave where the sullen prisoners were being held.

"It appears that you gentlemen already have the situation well in hand," he remarked. "Allow me to express my country's gratitude for what you have done. In due course, our government will also render its official thanks."

As the planes took off and soared homeward again, with Bronich and his henchmen on board, Tom heaved a sigh of relief.

"Oh, brother, am I glad to see the last of those Kranjovians!" he declared.

"Good riddance to bad rubbish, if you ask me!" muttered Chow. "Now let's all hotfoot it back to our own camp 'fore them reindeers start gallopin' over the place!"

"Reindeers?" said Tom. "You're a little mixed up, Chow. There are no reindeer at the South Pole."

"That's what you think, son." The cook chuckled.

"In case you ain't looked at the calendar lately, tonight's Christmas Eve!"

The next day there was a huge feast in the ice-cave mess hall at the American camp, which the men had decorated with green and red streamers and a papier-mâché Christmas tree.

Chow had outdone himself as chef. There was roast cold-storage turkey with chestnut dressing, cranberry sauce, and all the other trimmings. To top it all off, Chow brought on a huge, steaming plum pudding with hard sauce.

After all hands had stuffed themselves till they could hardly move, they joined in singing "Silent Night," "O Little Town of Bethlehem," and other Christmas carols.

But the best part of all was yet to come.

The radioman had rigged up a special short-wave hookup in the mess hall. Back in America, the friends and relatives of all the crew were standing by to wish them Merry Christmas!

Among the last voices to come on were those of Mr. and Mrs. Swift, who sent their good wishes to the boys and everyone else. "And now the girls have something to say," added Tom's mother.

"Good night! I sure hope Sandy remembered to get something nice for Phyl," Tom whispered to Bud.

"Oh, Tom!" Phyl's voice came over the loudspeaker. "The wrist watch you gave me is simply beautiful! I never realized you had such wonderful taste!"

"Well—uh—I thought you might like it," stammered Tom, as Bud chuckled softly.

By way of thanks, Phyl blew him a kiss into the mike, and Sandy did the same for Bud, after thanking him for the silver bracelet and earrings he had given her.

Then the boys opened their own presents, which Tom's family had sent along on Bud's cargo jet.

The following morning everyone rose early for the history-making event—the launching of the atomic earth blaster.

Tom had installed the drill's controls in one of the listening posts about two hundred yards from the launching platform. Set up in an ice cave, this was also the station to be used by Harold Voorhees for his thermal-measuring devices.

Fifty feet farther away, the other members of the expedition gathered in the snow to watch the proceedings through binoculars.

Equipped with earphones, Tom called for a last-minute report from the technical crew.

"Ready number one!" came a voice from the first listening post.

"Ready number two!"

"Ready number three!" said Voorhees.

"Ready seismology!" reported Dr. MacGregor, who was stationed in the radio cave to maintain contact with seismological and weather stations all over the world.

Tensely, Tom began to count over the mike:

"X minus five, four, three, two, one!"

Then he pushed a button and pulled down a lever. *The earth blaster whined into action!*

The young inventor glued his eye to a telescope trained on the launching platform atop a scaffold as high as a three-story building. As he watched, the blaster rapidly pierced the ice below and disappeared from view.

Moments later, reports began to come in from the listening posts. The blaster was working perfectly!

Voorhees put out his hand impulsively.

"Congratulations, Tom! Guess I've caused a lot of hard feeling because I lacked faith in your ability. But now my hat's off to you!"

Tom smiled as he shook hands with the blond scientist.

"Forget it. We've all been working under a strain, but now let's hope our troubles are over!"

As if in mockery of Tom's words, there was a sudden loud rumbling. The ice cave shook, and the ground seemed to quiver beneath them!

Tom's face went pale as he grabbed the control levers.

"I'm afraid we've hit a fault!" he cried.

Quickly he changed the operating direction of the blaster. But the rumbling continued!

Just then, Voorhees pointed out through the open doorway and gave a shout of alarm:

"Look!"

From the higher ground not far from the camp, small geysers of steam were rising. The next moment, the top of a nearby hill exploded, becoming a volcano of terrifying fury!

CHAPTER 25

## MOLTEN TRIUMPH

TRANSFIXED WITH HORROR, Tom and Voorhees stared at the volcano. Then they rushed from the listening post for a wider view of the catastrophe.

A column of smoke and gases billowed upward from the top of the cone, as red-hot cinders rained down in all directions! At the same time, the volcano spewed surge after surge of molten black lava, which came rolling down the hillside!

Striking the ice, the lava turned it instantly into hissing steam. Mingled with the acrid volcanic gases, this made the air almost unbreathable.

"Break out the gas masks!" Tom yelled to Bud Barclay. "Make sure every man gets one and wears it!"

"What do we do now, skipper?" demanded Arvid

Hanson tautly. "Seems to me as if that lava will bury the camp!"

Tom looked over the area, then shook his head. "I don't think so, Arv. I believe that formation of ice hummocks will deflect the stuff so the flow skirts our camp."

Tom's prediction was greeted with open doubts. Several of the men had fled from the camp in search of safer ground.

Without stopping to argue, Tom hurried back up the slope.

"Hey! Where in tarnation you goin', son?" Chow yelled after him.

"To call the listening posts!" Tom shouted back over his shoulder. In the control cave, he quickly made contact with Stations One and Two. In each case, the technicians reported that the outlook appeared safe so far, and that they planned to remain at their posts unless the situation changed.

When Tom returned, his men were huddled in an awe-struck group, watching the flood of boiling black lava creep closer and closer.

"Sure hope you know what you're talking about, blaster boy!" Bud muttered anxiously.

At first the terrifying ebony flood channeled itself around the camp. But suddenly part of the main stream branched off and forced a path through the hummocks. Roiling and boiling, it surged straight down toward the camp!

The men started to scatter in all directions, but Tom's voice stopped them in their tracks.

"Wait! It's slowing down! I think we're safe!"

The heat of the lava was so great now that it was melting deep puddles in the ice. The fuming black mass gradually sank down and buried itself in the gouges, leaving pools of hardened lava all over the landscape.

As the tide of lava subsided, Chow Winkler pulled down his gas mask and mopped his brow.

"Brand my galluses! Watchin' that stuff roll down on us is like fallin' off your bronco right smack in front o' a buffalo stampede!"

"The danger's over for the time being, but this may not be the last of it," warned Tom. "There could be another eruption!"

Several fearful hours crept by as everyone waited and watched for signs of another upheaval. Dr. Mac-Gregor, who had stuck to his post, reported there was no news of disturbances from any other part of the globe.

Finally Tom started back up the slope to the control cave to communicate again with the other listening posts. But part way up, he stopped and slapped his forehead with a groan of dismay.

"What's wrong?" exclaimed Bud, who was walking beside him.

"The blaster! I forgot to shut it off!"

"Holy smoke! By this time, it must be halfway to China!"

Breaking into a run, the boys dashed up to the control station. Inside the cave, Tom grabbed the signal tape that was steadily issuing from the electronic brain, and began to scan the loops and reels that had already fallen on the floor.

"Bud!" he shouted triumphantly. "The blaster's working perfectly! It's down five miles now!"

Pulling on the earphones, Tom established contact with Stations One and Two. The technical crews were still on the job. Then he sent Bud back to the camp again to recall Voorhees to his post.

All thought of the volcano was forgotten as Tom focused his attention on the progress of the blaster. Watching the dials carefully, he made occasional slight adjustments of the controls from time to time, as the electronic brain reeled out a steady record of the drill's progress.

Meanwhile, Voorhees was keeping check on the rising heat measurements as the blaster bored deeper and deeper into the earth.

Working in eight-hour shifts around the clock, Tom and his men kept track of the blaster as it dug deeper and deeper and deeper into the earth.

Five days later, Voorhees announced, "Two thousand degrees Fahrenheit, Tom!"

"Wow!" gasped Bud. "How deep is the blaster now, genius boy?"

"It's down over two hundred miles!" replied Tom.

A feeling of tension spread through the camp as the men gathered around the control post.

Suddenly Bud, who was standing in the open doorway, cried out, "Look! There she blows!"

No binoculars nor telescope was needed to see the white-hot geyser of molten iron that shot straight up in the air from the open shaft!

Tom's heart was hammering wildly. The sudden climax to his long months of work and planning left him dizzy and breathless with excitement. Above the cheers and clamor of the men, he could hear Bud shouting again and again:

"You've done it, Tom! You've done it!"

The gushing jet of molten iron made a white-hot arc as it plunged down into the hollowed-out artificial lake.

"What I wanna know is how d' you turn the stuff off, after you've got enough?" asked Chow in an awe-stricken voice.

"It ought to stop in a few minutes of its own accord," explained Tom. "As the metal cools, it'll seal off the hole made by the blaster, by forming a plug of solid iron."

But the flow seemed endless, and the level of metal inside the lake kept rising rapidly.

For a time there was fear that Tom's calculations about the time might be wrong—that the outpour

*Bud shouted again and again, "You've*

might continue indefinitely. But in twenty-five minutes the gush of molten iron dwindled and finally stopped, as though it had been choked off by the turning of a giant throttle.

*done it, Tom! You've done it!"*

Grabbing a long-handled ladle, Tom hurried to the lake to skim off some of the top layer of the tons of metal that had not yet completely congealed.

Then he rushed to his laboratory to analyze the sample.

"What's the verdict, skipper?" Bud asked.

"It's the purest sample of iron I've ever seen!" reported Tom excitedly.

The other men crowded around, clapping the young inventor on the back and congratulating him.

"Well, I didn't bankrupt Swift Enterprises, after all." Tom grinned. "But, brother, things sure had me worried for a while!"

Then he hurried off to the radio cave to report the outcome of the expedition to his father.

Mr. Swift was jubilant on hearing of his son's triumph.

"Tom, this is a stupendous scientific achievement! At a single stroke, you've added a whole new treasure house of iron to the world's resources! I almost hate to think what that'll mean when we hand out word to the press. Among other things, you'll be swamped with newsreel and television cameramen when the *Sky Queen* lands back here at Shopton!

"But hurry home, son, because we've all missed you! And besides"—he added with a chuckle—"I still need your help in figuring out that message from our space friends!"

After Tom signed off, Bud asked jokingly:

"Well, now that you've got all this iron, what are you going to do with it?"

Tom grinned, but considered the matter thoughtfully.

"Well, to begin with, I think Uncle Sam will allow us to tap just enough for Swift Enterprises to cover the cost of the expedition. After that, I believe the best plan will be to set up a world commission, with members from every nation, to control this new resource."

"You mean, let them decide how much every country will get and how much they should pay for it?"

"Right. After all, this molten iron is drawn off from under the whole earth's crust, so it should belong to the whole world—even though we just tapped it down here at the South Pole."

"Good deal," approved Bud admiringly.

At that moment Chow poked his head in the doorway and swung a dinner bell back and forth as he hollered:

"Soup's on, you two! And don't you go losin' your appetite, Tom, jest 'cause you struck it rich!"

The young inventor laughed. "No danger of that!"

As the boys headed for the mess hall, Bud asked, "What's our next objective, chum, after we wind up here? I'm still waiting for that interplanetary trip you and your dad keep talking about, to visit your space friends. How about that—from the South Pole to Mars!"

"Quite a jump, all right." Tom chuckled.

At this moment the young inventor was so thrilled with his present discovery that he did not let his mind wander far from it. But soon he was to become involved in another stirring project—*Tom Swift and His Outpost in Space*.

"Come on, let's celebrate!" Bud urged Tom. "Chow has a feast ready and I'm starved!"

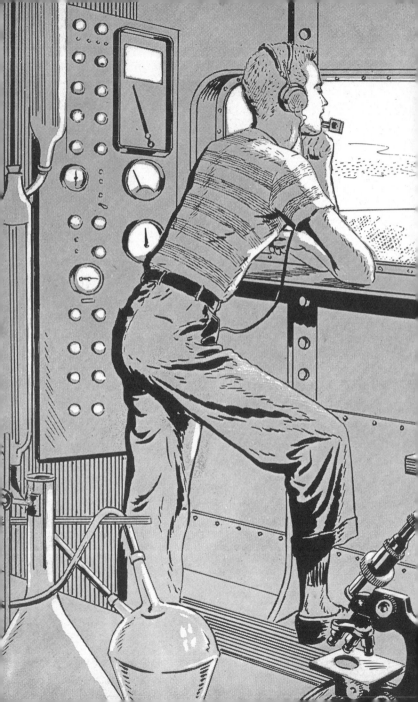